ANTHOLOGY ASKEW

VOLUME 007 - Nov 2019
ASKEW THRILLS

Published by

Rhetaskew Publishing

ISBN-13: 978-1-949398-29-8
ISBN-10: 1-949398-29-3

ANTHOLOGY ASKEW
Askew Thrills

Volume 007 – November 2019

<u>*fiction, poetry and artwork by*</u>

Melodie Corrigall ~ Adam Johnson
Lynn White ~ Jim Tritten ~ Wim Verveen
Laurie Kolp ~ P. A. O'Neil ~ Maxwell Zwain
John Grey ~ Phil Gladden ~ Nerisha Kemraj
Ed Ahern ~ Faith Maria Brody ~ Patricia Walkow
Steve Carr ~ Mandy Melanson ~ Michelle Murray
Ron Wilson ~ Dusty Grein ~ Sandi Hoover
Ben Graham ~ Kent Swarts ~ Nikki Rohira
Kimberly Garrett Brown ~ Sarah Henry

Contents

Welcome Back

Mandy Melanson

Wow! Has it really been over a year since we last saw each other? It has...

In the year we've been away, we brought 7 novels, 3 poetry collections, and 2 limited edition anthologies into the Askewverse. This surge of creativity from like-minded authors helped us realize that our mission, while noble, was short-sighted. Askew was created not simply to help authors become better writers, but to spread positivity and community—one story at a time.

Since opening Askew to novelists, we've seen our authors spread their community based positive message with the masses. We've also seen them strive to quite literally change the world as they tackle sensitive social and political issues. They have been consistently welcomed to Barnes and Noble for book signings, and even considered for awards from PEN to Lambda Literary. We could not be more proud of our Askew authors.

One thing was missing though...

We missed the anthologies that started the Askew library. We missed helping new authors hone their skills and improve their craft. We missed seeing the camaraderie between seasoned authors and those just breaking into the industry. So... we're back!

This time we're bringing you the thrills and chills to remind you exactly why we're Askew in the first place. Once you turn the page, you're in for a roller coaster ride of emotions; one we hope you won't soon forget.

About This Volume

Dusty Grein

Hey there Askew readers.

For this anthology, we asked our authors to thrill us, and they didn't disappoint. Thrills can mean different things to different folks, and when you are Askew, you never know what you will discover when you look.

In these pages, you will find action, adventure, romance, fear, and a host of writing that spans genres and styles. From hard-hitting fantasy with a half-dragon hero, to diabolical science fiction, where the plot twists will grab you and never let go. The ride includes a little of everything, from the thrills of a rediscovered lost love, to the chills of scientific experiment gone horribly awry.

I think it is only fair to let you know that there ARE some very strong and explicitly narrated stories inside. If you are easily frightened, or squeamish, you may want to find a hand to hold as you proceed.

Be sure you watch out for those sharp corners, and if I were you, I would double check that seatbelt before we take off.

Ready?

Good! Here we go . . .

Just a Girl

Michelle Murray

As I walk outside
Under the big blue sky
Watching the clouds roll by
The sun on my face
Its rays beaming down on me
I realize
I'm just a girl
In this big wide world
A small figure
Walking along
A speck of dust
In this wide world of space
This road I'm on
Just a small part
Of the vast universe
Filled with gases, stars,
planets, and such
And here I am
Walking
Wondering
What my place is
Just a girl
Walking along.

Come Hither

Dusty Grein

I had no idea how long she had been watching me. In fact, I wasn't even sure what time it was when I first noticed her, sitting with her back against the stained marble door to the mausoleum.

I had been sitting alone in the graveyard for quite a while, and the moon had traveled at least three-fourths of the way across the starry sky. For a long time, there had been only dry, dead leaves on the cracked steps leading to the crypt; then all at once she was there, although I wasn't sure how. The only thing I was certain of, was that I had never seen such a beautiful but intensely scary woman in my life.

My first thought was, she must be one of the sorority chicks from school, but the way she moved her hand provocatively across her chest and unbuttoned the top of her blouse was too mature, too practiced, too designed, for her to have been an undergrad. My initiation into the Fraternal Order of the League of Crypt-Minders was almost over, and the thought she might ruin my acceptance passed through my mind, but only for a fleeting instant.

I turned to face her and held my candle-lantern up higher.

Her eyes sparkled in the flickering light, and her smile commanded my full attention. She ran her tongue around her lips, and I felt myself go hard. The fact that her top teeth seemed too long and too sharp wasn't enough to overcome the raw lust that seemed to ooze from those lips. She seemed to know the effect she had on me, and her eyes traveled to the obvious erection that was becoming more and more uncomfortable by the second. I tried to move and found that other than my eyes, I was unable to control a single muscle in my body. She pulled her bent legs closer to her chest, then let her feet slide as far apart as she could. Slowly she spread her knees, and her skirt slid down from her knees, inching its way along impossibly smooth and creamy thighs, settling into the spot where her torso met the ground between her legs.

There it rustled, as if in a slight breeze, playing peek-a-boo with my mind, providing tantalizing glimpses at promised mysteries and elusive folds of flesh, just out of sight.

My eyes traveled back up toward her face, but only made it as far as the swell of her small, firm breasts. Dimly glimpsed in the flickering light, visibly erect nipples strained against the sheer fabric of her blouse.

The constriction in my pants had grown unbearable, and a dull ache traveled down into the depth of my testicles.

They felt like twenty-pound weights had been tied to them, and the sound of her soft laughter sent chills down my spine.

I wanted her, and she knew it.

She slowly moved her hand from her knee, down her thigh, one finger drawing ever closer to the shadowy spot that had become my sole focus, my only purpose.

It was then that I noticed her fingers.

They didn't seem to match the rest of her, and were in fact bony. Each swollen knuckle was bent at a strange angle, so that none of them seemed normal. I felt an instant of fear, and as I did, her whole image shimmered.

Where she had been seated, there now sat a wizened crone, with shriveled skin and strings of graying hair. Gone were the sexy blouse and skirt. The ancient witch was nude; her wrinkly flaps of breasts lay with elongated and flat nipples across a bloated stomach. My eyes traveled down past the sagging belly to a wiry nightmare of gray hair, and God-help-me, what looked like small writhing snakes. I felt my eyes grow wide as I helplessly looked back up, into that hideous face.

She waved one of her skeletal hands in the air, and just like that she was back. The gorgeous young woman, impossibly erotic, in an altogether mind-blowing portrayal of raw sexuality and desire. "Sorry about that, my pet," she said in a voice of liquid honey. "I'll try not to slip like that again. At least not until, after."

From the depths of my animal-brain, I felt only a white-hot desire to touch, to taste, to penetrate and to be consumed by whatever fate she had in store. My reasoning mind wanted to scream, but seemed to be detached from the body that now betrayed me.

The ache in my groin, the pulse in my swollen member, and the hunger in her eyes made my feet move forward of their own accord. In terror, I watched myself take another step closer to my doom . . .

My Mother's Words

Laurie Kolp

A picture is worth
a thousand words.

And any word is worth
a mountain

because muddy molehills
don't show up in pictures,

nor do they appear as
pretty as a picture of
purple mountaintops.

Your filthy words aren't
sticks and stones
breaking my bones,
but they still hurt me.

I feel as dumb as
a box of rocks

when you say
what doesn't kill me
makes me stronger.

It's as if everything
that's happened,

my whole damn life,

has been taken
with a grain of salt.

Salt of the earth,
your words replay
a thousand pictures
in my mind.

Like a
broken record,

bones
beneath this
fucking mound
of dirt.

Sir Thomas Bondo

Patricia Walkow

Sir Thomas Bondo settled himself on his haunches, covering the young girl's torso. He yawned long and wide then stretched his full length on the girl, as she lay on her back in bed drifting toward sleep. His luxurious fluffy black tail draped down her legs, his front paws framed each side of her neck, and he rested his broad head beneath her chin.

Every night Bondo's young mistress ran her hand along his glossy fur and she played the same game. If she touched an area on her cat's back, would it be a white section of fur, or black? She knew her cat so well, she was usually correct when she looked where her hand rested on his body. All Bondo did was nuzzle more deeply into her and purr. They fell asleep sharing their breath.

Sir Thomas Bondo was undisputedly *her* cat. Not her mother's, and not her father's, who lived in a distant city. She had been devoted to her large neutered male companion since he was adopted as a stray kitten. Now, five years later, the cat and girl were as close as any cat and girl could be, and he was as protective of his young charge as a lioness would be of her cubs. The girl's mother occasionally remarked that all seventeen pounds of him—every strand of his semi-long fur, and every inch of his long white whiskers—were in love with *his* girl. His sharp nails were clipped by the girl's mom now and then, but he always retracted them for his family. Neither Lupe nor her mother had ever felt the pain of a razor-sharp claw, or wickedly long fang.

If it weren't for Sir Thomas Bondo, Lupe knew she would be a very lonely ten-year-old, because of the wine-colored birthmark circling her left eye and temple, like half of a mask. She thought that maybe Bondo couldn't see it, or maybe he just didn't care about it, since it never caused him to shy away from her.

Mask-Face was just one of the cruel nicknames some of the other youngsters hurled at her—the moniker which had been initiated and promoted by Lupe's nemesis, Becky. There were other epithets like Purple-Face, Half-Raccoon, and Blotch-Eye; but Mask-Face is the bullying name that stuck. It was the one Becky, who lived six houses away, insisted on using. She coerced the other kids to use it as well, by telling them she wouldn't be their friend anymore if they didn't.

Lupe and Becky were in the same fifth-grade class, but they may as well have been from different planets. Becky was blonde and hip, very popular, and always surrounded by an orbit of other girls, like satellites. Girls who might have been Lupe's friends, if Becky allowed it. Girls who were afraid to cross Becky. Girls who decided not to attend Lupe's tenth birthday party, after Becky convinced them they shouldn't be seen with freaky Mask-Face.

It didn't matter that Lupe was pretty, despite the birthmark. Her features were symmetrical, her hair was a long, rich, reddish-brown, and her mouth was a perfect shape. Her brain, too, was beautiful—agile and quick—and Lupe was engaged in her studies.

Becky, on the other hand, was an average student and her mother allowed her to do anything she wanted. That's probably why, at ten years old, Becky had tricolor hair. Her mother had dyed it, so Becky's stringy, blonde hair was pink at the bottom of each strand, white in the middle, and green at the end. It reminded Lupe of spumoni, and she privately called Becky Spumoni-Head.

Lupe told her mom about the nickname, but her mother said she should not use nasty nicknames for others.

"But what about what they call me? You know, Mask-Face. Isn't that nasty, too?" Lupe complained.

"The kids are wrong to call you that. Don't be like them." Mom looked at the cat. "Isn't that right, Sir Thomas?

The cat blinked his eyes a few times.

"I want to get this ugly birthmark removed, Mom!"

"Lupe, we have talked about this already. It can't be removed until you are older. You are still growing. In the meantime, we can cover it with makeup. Don't worry about what anyone calls you. You know how pretty you are, and how smart you are." Mom bent down and smoothed the cat's fur. "And Sir Thomas knows, too."

Bondo pushed his head into the woman's hand.

When the cat had first arrived, Lupe and her mother named him "Thomas" but then decided "Sir Thomas" was more distinguished. A year after he arrived, Lupe's mother had commented to her how bonded Sir Thomas was to her.

"What does 'bonded' mean, Mom?" a then six-year-old Lupe had asked.

"It means you and Sir Thomas love each other and want to be together."

Lupe thought about what her mom said and then announced. "I think I am going to call him 'Bondo' from now on."

Mom had smiled. "Then it's official. His full name is 'Sir Thomas Bondo' as of right now."

As Lupe grew, her cat followed her to the end of the driveway each morning, where she waited for the school bus, and he met her at the end of the driveway each afternoon when she returned. It didn't matter if it was hot or cold, sunny, raining, snowing, or windy. Bondo was always there for Lupe.

He sat on the kitchen table while she did her homework, and each night they slept together, coordinating their breathing and the rhythm of their hearts, warming each other with their bodies, and falling asleep nose-to-nose. His breath was hers and her breath was his.

~

On the last day of fifth-grade, the bus dropped off Lupe and Spumoni-Head in front of Lupe's driveway. As Becky walked away toward her house, she shouted, "Have a great summer, Mask-Face . . . with your stupid, ugly cat. Too bad you don't have any friends!"

Bondo walked onto the sidewalk and sat still, watching Becky walk to her house, and staring intently as she climbed the few steps to her front door. His tail twitched on the concrete, then thumped twice, hard.

He turned to accompany Lupe on the driveway.

As he approached her, she bent down and picked him up, burying her face in his neck. Her cheeks were wet. "You are not stupid, Bondo. You are my smart cat. I love you."

Bondo looked at her and blinked his eyes, turned his head to face the direction of Becky's house, and hissed.

~

A few days later, Lupe rode her bike up and down the driveway and then she ventured to ride on the street. She dreaded passing Becky's house.

Stupid Becky . . . question is more what color will your hair be when school starts again? I hope it's green . . . then I'll call you Spinach Scalp.

Sir Thomas Bondo waited on the lawn next to the end of the driveway where it met the sidewalk. It wasn't long before he saw Lupe being chased by Becky. Becky's bike was newer and faster.

Lupe couldn't outride her.

Becky got so close, Lupe crashed onto the lawn, while Becky rode away sing-songing, "Mask-Face, Mask-Face, you can't ride a bike with grace . . . Mask-Face, Mask-Face, it's all because of your ugly face!"

The fall caused a few scrapes on Lupe's knees and arms, but the deeper hurt was the way Spumoni-Head always tried to insult her.

Bondo came over to Lupe and licked her face. He walked back to the middle of the sidewalk and headed about fifty feet toward Becky's house.

"Bondo, come back! Don't go there," Lupe called. She didn't trust Becky not to hurt him.

He sat at the sound of Lupe's voice, but flicked his tail right and left with sharp movements, then slapped it hard on the concrete. He squinted and quietly chattered, the way cats do when seeing a bird or mouse.

He returned to Lupe's side, and together they went into the house; Bondo didn't bother waiting for Lupe to open the door to the kitchen, slipping inside through his pet door instead.

Since Mom was still at work, Lupe attended to her wounds with soap and warm water, then some antibiotic cream and a bandage. When she was done, she sat on the sofa and cried for an hour.

Bondo jumped up to be with her. He settled in her lap, licked her tears, and put his front paws around her familiar neck, rubbing his head against his girl's cheeks and marking her with his scent.

"I am so glad I have you," Lupe gasped through ragged breaths.

Bondo jumped down and headed toward his pet door. He stopped just short of it, then pivoted toward the water bowl to take a few sips. He looked at the pet door again, rumbled out a low growl, but trotted to Lupe and settled at her feet.

He looked up at her and flicked his eyelids closed for a second, turned his face back toward the pet door, then lifted his right paw to his face. He cleaned it and then started working on his left paw before spending the next twenty minutes giving himself a complete bath, as though preparing for a photo shoot. Or maybe just a long nap.

Lupe watched TV before she set the table for supper. Sir Thomas Bondo did not let her out of his sight; where she went, he followed. A few times he had stopped and stared at his pet door, but trailed her back to the living room. He used his scratching post while she was occupied by a program.

After Lupe fell asleep that night, the cat quietly left her side, slipped through his pet door, and proceeded directly to Becky's house. He had made this middle-of-the-night trek three times in the last ten days, while Lupe was in deep REM sleep, completely unaware her pet was on the prowl. Bondo made sure he avoided the band of long-clawed raccoons in the neighborhood. They could be trouble, so he steered clear of the alleys where they noisily raided trashcans.

He sat at the base of the large, sprawling tree, as he had on each of his previous excursions. It climbed past Becky's second story window; being summer, she kept that window open at night.

Bondo knew the open window belonged to her; he had seen her on his previous visits. Tonight, however, would be different. Tonight, he would climb the tree.

He stretched every muscle and stood tall on his hind legs as he sharpened his claws on the tree, and then sprayed the tree with urine. This was followed by more claw sharpening, and a bit more cleaning his toes.

Finally, he sat still and simply stared at the open window; his only movement, that of his uncontrollable restless tail.

With one jump he made a perfect leap to the first cleft in the tree, and scrambled up the branch, which took him within a foot of Becky's open window. He easily gauged his next jump, and landed without a sound on her windowsill.

~

Lupe and her mother were jolted awake by a posse of screaming sirens. They grabbed their robes and ran to the end of the driveway. From here they could see a snarl of fire trucks, police cars, and an ambulance at Becky's house.

"What do you think happened, Mom?"

"I don't know, Honey."

Some other neighbors stood near them, and one of the women in the group had rushed to Becky's house as the emergency vehicles arrived. She said, "Becky was attacked while she was sleeping."

Lupe's mouth flung open, shocked.

"Who would do that?" Lupe's mom asked, raising her trembling voice, upset there might be a predator in the neighborhood.

"They think it was some kind of animal," the woman said.

Lupe and her mom watched as Becky was placed in the ambulance, her face wrapped in bloody towels. They stayed glued to the sidewalk until the ambulance wailed away.

"Tomorrow, I'll try to find out what really happened, and how Becky is," her mom said. "In the meantime, we will lock our doors all the time, even during the daytime. Do you understand, Lupe?"

"Yes, Mom. I'll keep the doors locked when I leave the house."

"And when you are in the house, too."

"OK, Mom. I'll lock the doors."

Bondo won't let anything happen to me, Lupe thought as they headed back into the house. *But he is just a cat; maybe we need a dog someday.*

Once in the house, they found Sir Thomas in the kitchen, licking his toes and nails with his sandpaper tongue and rubbing his saliva-moistened paws against his face.

Lupe thought she saw a strand of colorful hair on his whiskers, but before she could reach down and grab it, he wiped his face with the side of his paw, and swallowed the hair.

She froze. *Did Bondo hurt Becky?* Lupe whispered to the cat, "I hope Becky is going to be OK."

Bondo continued washing himself.

"Come on Bondo, let's go back to bed," Lupe called to him.

Sir Thomas Bondo bounded up the stairs to Lupe's room, while doctors tended to spumoni-haired Becky, whose face was severely lacerated and bitten, from above her left eye to below her temple.

As the seventeen-pound cat jumped on Lupe's bed with an affectionate "Brrr", the emergency room doctor told Becky and her mother that the scars would fade, but probably not disappear. It might have been a raccoon, or maybe a stray cat—since no one knew what had attacked Becky, she would need to have a series of painful rabies shots.

Bondo softly padded to Lupe, clambered onto her chest, sprawled his body to cover the length of her trunk and thighs, and extended his long front legs so his soft, gentle paws embraced the sides of her neck.

Lupe placed her hand on a spot on his body and guessed if it was white or black. When she checked her guess, she was right. She whispered to her cat, "Did your hurt Becky?"

Sir Thomas Bondo opened his mouth wide in an extended, luxurious yawn, and turned his head upside down against her neck. Lupe turned off the nightstand light.

She started to doze off as she stroked his fur, but when he settled his nose against hers, the image of the tri-color hair he swallowed made Lupe's heart pound.

It made her smile, too, just a little bit. *What if Bondo really had done something to Becky?*

She sat up as fear overtook her—fear it was true, and fear for her cat's life if he was guilty. As much as she hated Becky, she didn't want her classmate to be injured . . . at least not by Bondo.

Lupe picked up the cat and buried her face in his tummy. The cat licked her hair as though it was his own fur.

She settled into her pillow, and the cat draped himself over her once again. She whispered, "Bondo, if you did hurt Becky, I'll never tell . . . not ever. It will be our secret."

Bondo relaxed every muscle and melted into her, before he exploded into a deep, noisy purr. He nuzzled his nose against hers, and they both fell asleep, nostril-to-nostril.

His breath was hers, and her breath was his.

Mr. X

John Grey

I live with vermin.
No wonder I'm as much
pestilence as anything else
in the sewer.

Survival is my holy grail.
So I creep around,
feeding here, stealing there,
keep to the pipes, the shadows.

They say that if you see a rat
then there's twenty you don't see.

So that creak you can't explain,
the wheeze that sounds like breathing,
the scraping between the walls....
let them be by way of introduction.

The Alternative

Dusty Grein

Rialla knew her family would miss her, but in all reality, they had lost her already. She hoped and prayed the old witch had told her the truth. Her mind was mind up; one way or another, this would be the last day she spent in this hell.

She gave up all of her dreams to secure her family's future. Her father cried the day she left; she had never seen him do that before. The pain in her heart had almost stopped her feet that day, but the incredible promise of Lord Mandarallen's agreement kept her resolve from crumbling.

Like her entire family, Rialla was born into servitude. Now, by agreeing to become one of Mandarallen's concubines, she secured freedom for her family, and enough land for them to support themselves as free folk, even though she would no longer be with them to enjoy it. Sometimes you have to lose everything, to gain what matters most.

She had thought she could do it—move to a fancy room in the Lord's manor, dress in the softest silk, and eat only the finest food. That was, until the first night she had been forced to endure his twisted passions. The humiliation of the things he had made her do . . . she seriously contemplated jumping from the parapet of the tower she now slept in, despite the threat of eternal damnation that came with suicide.

Yesterday, as she wandered depressed through the cold, dim halls of the manor, Rialla met the witch. The pity the old woman showed her was either a blessing or a curse.

Soon, she would know for sure.

"Perhaps there is yet another way out," the witch told her, in a voice as rough as sandpaper. "If you are willing to give up everything you have left, including any chance to ever see your family again."

For someone ready to die, just to escape, that was an easy choice.

As the sky darkened, she made her way into the loft of the horse barn, where she found a huge pile of feathers, just as the witch said she would. She breathed deeply, said a silent farewell to the world, sat down, and opened the bag.

In a shaft of silver moonlight, Rialla lay back in the downy softness and let the small vial roll from her numb fingers. The incantation had gone well, and the stone had turned blue in her hand, as the old woman had said it would. She hoped the end—and the beginning—would be painless. This too was a promise from the witch, but one that had been said with much less conviction.

The last thing Rialla saw as her eyes fluttered shut, was the large tawny owl which swooped in and landed next to her head. She blinked twice and as her eyes closed, her shallow breathing slowed to a stop, and her body released her.

~

For what seemed like hours she fought the crushing panic she felt. Her fear threatened to drag her away into darkness, yet bit by bit she clawed her way up, toward the flattened face of the bird; it was so close, yet so far away. With a final push, she used the last of her strength to send herself hurtling toward that face, directly at the sharp beak and huge eyes of the predator.

The universe echoed a resounding silent scream and her mind snapped over that of the owl, twisting into the form it now must occupy inside the creature.

She blinked its [*her*] large eyes, intrigued by the difference in the color spectrum it [*she*] could see. The animal brain was still strong, even though it was under her will.

She [*it*] was hungry.

Looking down at the cooling corpse by her feet, she let the instinct to feed take control. The only thing sweeter than the relief her new body felt at being fed, was the taste of the human blood dripping from the chunks of meat as she devoured them.

Parasailing Date

Laurie Kolp

When you say we might die if we fall
I assume you mean into the water
not in love. Here we are, gliding like gulls
when you say we might die if we fall.

From this high, I hear the speedboat's squall
while whitecaps wave below as if aware
you are saying we might die if we fall,
assuming you mean into the water.

Like Father, Like Daughter

Wim Verveen

Ice-cold wind bit at the skin of the man treading carefully along the tiny ridge, glued to the side of the ravine. The wall stretched downward for an eternity, before disappearing into darkness. It would easily challenge the deepest ravines found on the old Earth, a place few remembered.

Earth had become only a shimmer of its former glory, torn by wars and pollution. The planet was finally abandoned by the last survivors, in a desperate attempt to escape the man made hell, after the rape and pillage of the last fruits of Gaia.

Mankind spread to the stars forming new civilizations, new nations. With that spread came new problems, and new wars. Humans never changed.

One of the descendants of those original colonists, was George Harris, the man currently on the ridge, defying certain death in the eternal cold winter of the small planet of Kaisus III. Found and colonized in the year 548 after the great departure, it provided little comfort to its inhabitants.

George however liked this place.

It was quiet, simple and harsh. Exactly the way he preferred life to be. George was a highly decorated former general in the armed forces of the West Beyond, who had settled down here on Kaisus III after his retirement.

He was alone. His wife was long gone, a subject he tended to avoid mentioning. The ridge led him to a small path. Undeterred by the growing gale, he proceeded toward a group of scattered buildings, gathered around a flat surface

with a small control tower. The tower was the only sign that those living here were, in fact, a nation of space faring people.

A few hangers covered in snow, hid their ships from the elements, and a road led north to the mines, where precious ores were acquired. This was really the only reason anyone wanted to be here; everyone that is, except George, who took the same walk every day, hunting for the few creatures who managed to live in this place.

~

The door slammed shut behind him as he entered. Immediately, snow crystals began to melt as the heaters automatically kicked in and brought the inside of the house above freezing. George put his gear away and left an oddly formed animal on the kitchen counter.

He poured himself a drink, before he sat down in the only chair the small house possessed. The glass had almost reached his lips when he stopped. He was highly aware, and his eyes had detected an anomaly. A small light was blinking on the communication panel off to one side; an indication of an incoming message.

George had never received a message. Not once, since he arrived many years ago. In fact, he never used the communication equipment at all.

He sat motionless in the chair for over a standard hour before he pushed a button to activate the panel. A screen lit up and took it's time to start. Finally a menu appeared, and a single line in his inbox.

His glass fell on the floor and shattered.

George stared at the name of the sender, then shook his head as if he was trying to remove his thoughts.

No.

This . . . this couldn't be true. "Anna." The word died on his lips. How many years had it been since he had spoken her name?

The image, which still haunted his dreams, came alive in his mind. The small child playing in uniform in the living room. The sound of laughter, which he craved to hear again.

Anna Harris, his daughter.

He had raised her alone after her mother died; she was a troubled kid, but he had always tried his best to keep her in line and teach her military skills. Toys were for the weak—he had never had them himself, and he had seen no reason to change that practice. She had rebelled time and time again, while they moved from assignment to assignment—from space stations, to moon-bases, or sometimes even a planet-side installation.

One day, after he returned from an exercise, she was gone. He had been devastated.

A deep pain came alive in his stomach, as his memories escaped from where he had hidden them; his eyes began to glisten. Anna was only sixteen when she left, but she had managed to crack his vault and take his money.

One of his teams was on it right away, but she had covered her tracks well. By the time they located her, she was already gone with a cargo vessel, and she never arrived at the destination, where they waited for her.

After that, the military wasn't quite the same for George. A few years later he resigned and retreated to this isolated place. With a deep sigh, he opened the message.

So she was still alive; he had always wondered. He stopped breathing when he began to read, but his heart quickly went into overdrive, and sweat travelled along his spine. The message contained only one word, but that one word was enough. He was immediately out of his chair and retrieving his old gear from a locked closet in the bedroom. The screen continued to display its one-word message. "Help."

~

"Mark, I need you to trace a message. Now."

A sloppy looking guy in a worn uniform sprang up as George entered the small shack next to the interstellar communication installation.

'Yes Sir, I mean, George. What do you want me to trace?"

He wasn't much younger than George, few words were exchanged. George handed him a data card which disappeared into one of the many machines which took up most of the space in the shack. Humming, the man began to operate the computer, which displayed a visual track of the message route on a large screen. Several connected dots appeared ending in one dot with a small description.

Mark whistled. "That place is no good, no good at all sir."

"Ready my vessel. I want to be off planet within the hour."

"But, Sir?"

"Was I somehow unclear, Sergeant?"

"Within the hour, Sir. I'll get right on it."

The ship's cabin smelled vaguely of rocket fuel, but George ignored it as he watched the instruments. The violent vibrations associated with the ascent slowed down, and the stars welcomed him, making his heart settle down for the first time since he had read the message.

He entered the destination in the nav computer and took the atmospheric engines offline. For a moment he sat in his chair; one screen still displayed the message—just the one word and her name on top. He tapped the worn plasma rifle next to his seat. "We are going on a trip, I might need you old friend."

He raised himself and activated the controls. A new vibration travelled through the ship. His vision blurred and for a few seconds all his senses went haywire. When his body returned to normal he looked at the navcomputer's screen.

A path to the target was now set, and a number slowly decreased. He closed his eyes and relaxed his muscles; he still had a long way to go.

~

"There you are." George watched the small speck hanging above the planet. "Targaz V, the hellhole of the galaxy, maybe even the universe." The station, with the same name as the planet it orbited, grew quickly on the screen.

His fingers tapped on the protective cover of the weapons control panel, while keeping an eye on his detection screen. Far away there were several ships en route, but none were identified as a threat.

A warning sound grabbed his attention, as a red light began flashing and several red dots appeared on the screen. The speaker began spouting an abomination of the language, which was barely decipherable. Hopefully the protocol hadn't changed too much.

George activated his communication panel, and began uploading the requested data. It took several seconds before he received an acknowledgement, and the red dots turned to white again.

~

His ship touched down at the designated spot in the station's landing array. Outside, a few figures approached and waited for him to disembark.

"I'm the harbor master. I need to ask about your weapons . . ."

Their handshake was almost as firm as the money in George's hand.

". . . but, I'm sure you have a permit for those. Refuel the ship?"

The harbor master quickly slid his hand into an inner pocket on his coat. He ordered his men to fetch a large refueling hose.

George was already on his way to the center of the station. The control room looked more like a barbarian cave, than the high tech center of a space station. In the middle of the cavernous space, sat a large man with tattoos covering his bare arms and chest, staring at George. One of the several guards approached him.

"You cannot bring this in he—ah!"

The guard fell to the floor, his nose broken. The large man hadn't moved a muscle, but several guards now had their weapons at the ready.

Calmly, George took up a position opposite the man who was obviously in charge.

"You have some nerve showing up here Fleet admiral Harris."

"That was long ago, Robert. I see you've moved up in the world. Love what you've done to the place."

"Well, that is mostly thanks to you. After a tactical retreat I encountered this rusty piece of shit hanging in space, and I stayed. Somehow, nobody came after me, and here I am."

"I remember your retreat; you were just lucky I had distractions." George's expression grew stern. "You will allow me free access to this station Robert . . . or else."

"You moron. Why would I ever even consider such humiliation?"

"Because, my dear fellow, I may no longer be a Fleet admiral, but I do still have friends in high places. Do you want to keep this taped-together contraption, or would you like to meet the Prime Fleet of the West Beyond?"

Robert's face grew red as he stared at George's dark smile. "Fine. Do whatever you need, but if your not off my station in 24 hours, I will come for you, regardless of your connections."

~

Twenty four hours, on a station the size of a small city. *Not gonna be easy to find a girl in a place like this*, he thought when he entered the twentieth bar.

This one was possibly the worst of the lot. Scantily clad girls moved between bad smelling spacefaring crewmen, all the while being watched by two impressive guards stationed next to the door, their weapons visible.

"Anna? No, never heard of her."

The bartender left him and attended to another client. *Another dead end.* In a way he was glad, this wasn't a place for his girl at all.

He made his way to the restroom through a semi-dark hallway, with only a vague reminder of paint on the wall, hidden below countless haphazardly glued on flyers.

Just below one of the lights, a torn poster drew his attention.

Settimo's Retreat, true relaxation for every man.

The picture above this line was partially obscured by other posters. George pulled them away to see the relaxing scenery. One face among the "merchandise" drew his attention.

"Oh my god, Anna!"

~

The establishment was classy, compared to some of the joints he had been in. He checked his communicator; time was ticking. A last glance outside before he closed the door. The same people he had seen milling around before, were still there and preoccupied with looking everywhere except at him. How long would it be before they found out there was no fleet coming?

"Welcome guest. I'm Settimo. Let me get your coat, and please, take a seat while I arrange for a viewing of our merchandise."

George eyed the guard for a moment, before he turned his attention to the owner and the few people present in the main room. He began to unbutton his coat.

Settimo stepped forward to take the coat, and George head-butted the man, flooring him immediately. The guard reached for his gun, but a moment too late. George was already aiming his own weapon at the guard's face, and proceeded to chain him to a nearby pole with his own handcuffs.

George began methodically checking the rooms and rounding up the unsuspecting occupants; Anna was nowhere to be seen.

"Where is she?"

'What . . . who? My head hurts."

"Trust me, a whole lot of other body parts will be hurting if you don't tell me where Anna is."

"Who is Anna?"

"Don't give me that, asshole. Here, look at this. This is on your own poster."

"Oh, you mean Candy. Ouch! I think you broke my nose!"

Geaorge rapped the man on top of the head with his sidearm. "My daughter, where is she?"

"I don't know! Please, don't hurt me. I . . . I sold her."

"To who? Tell me who you sold her to, or your kneecaps are going to be one less thing you have to worry about."

"No, please! All I know is that he is a trader from Victory Station. I'm speaking the truth!"

"Victory Station? Really? I will be back if you're lying."

"I am telling the honest truth, Sir." The man jumped up. "Wait, before you leave. She left some items, maybe you want those?"

Settimo hurried into a back room, then came back quickly and handed George a worn bag. He immediately recognized it. Anna had been here, there was no doubt; he had given her this bag on her 16th birthday.

He grabbed the bag and checked it's contents. Skipping through some odds and ends, he found a picture on the bottom.

His picture.

A small, crumpled photograph, the corner worn down, as if someone had held it intensely for many hours, or maybe days. To George's surprise, his eyes began to sting yet again. He took a deep breath while he imagined her holding it.

He caught a sudden movement out of the corner of his eye, and ducked, just in time. An energy beam hit the door behind him.

His reaction was immediate, and Settimo collapsed on the floor, blood spreading out around him. This wasn't good.

George quickly exited through the back of the building and made his way through the cramped street.

~

He sighed loudly with relief when his ship left the bay, and moved into space. He set his course and ignited the main engines.

He was lucky so far, but they would find the body any moment now, and he had to run before they launched interceptors.

Victory Station, of all places. Why did she have to be there?

Satisfied the ship was managing its course, he grabbed his daughters bag and retreated to the small crew area, where he emptied it on the table. There was nothing important in it, other than the photograph.

Hastily he began preparing some coffee, ignoring an inner urge to let his emotions take over. As he drank the hot liquid, he focused on feeling it burn his lips and the feelings subsided. A decorated officer, he could never let those emotions take control. There was only one important thing—the mission. He sat down on his bed, remembering Anna, just before she left.

A second memory surfaced. A woman with those same features, but older. He clenched his hands together trying to make this memory go away, but the images and emotions only grew stronger. He had failed so many times; first losing her, then their daughter. Why?

~

"Ma'am, the approaching ship checks out. Shall I let it through?"

"Wait."

The woman who spoke was hardly visible in the semi dark of the room. On screen, the ship grew in size as it came nearer. Several seconds passed before the woman bent forward and changed the threat code.

"But Ma'am, that ship isn't—"

"You have your orders. Deal with the situation."

The guard began keying in commands.

Far below, a red light began blinking in the hangar, and a squad of security troops hurried onto the platform as the ship made its final descent into its designated spot.

Without warning, a loud bang, audible in the shielded control room, tore through the air. Flames and smoke erupted from a nearby freighter.

A second blast from the arriving ship burned holes in a second freighter, sending shockwaves towards the approaching soldiers.

"This is getting out of hand. What should I do? Ma'am?"

The guard looked behind him, but there were only shadows.

~

George watched the uniformed men filing onto the landing platform. A cold crept up his spine; this was not normal procedure. His ship had military codes, they should be happy with his arrival. Still holding the controls, he began unbuckling his seatbelt and readied his gun. Whoever was in charge of Victory Station now, was clearly in the pocket of the ones who had taken his daughter.

Quickly George tapped some in a few final commands, then ran to the airlock. The vehicle shuddered and threw him to the side; he barely managed to continue. As he reached the airlock controls, the ship swept sideways.

The door opened, luckily there were no soldiers on this side of the platform. He jumped out and was quickly obscured by smoke. He blasted a hole in a maintenance hatch and lowered himself into a tube, leading to one of the maintenance corridors.

There were benefits to knowing the entire layout of this station. In the dim maintenance lighting, he hastily made his way through the corridors, as if he had spent his entire life here. It was warm and moist down here. The persistent noises of machinery made it impossible to hear anything else.

Finally he halted before an exit where most of the paint had rusted away. A code panel lit up when he came close. He tried a memorized code, and the door gave a metallic groan as it released the locks and swung open. George shook his head. "Security expectations have clearly suffered since my days here."

He stripped off his spacesuit, revealing an inconspicuous overall, then retrieved a coat from the bag containing his gun. Slowly he stepped out and found himself in a deserted hallway; debris was piled up along the sides, and the floor was so dusty he left a trail behind him.

The hallway ended at a simple metal door, but this control panel was dead. George unscrewed the panel, revealing a manual control handle. Carefully, he worked the handle back and forth several times, before it finally gave in.

The sounds of people greeted him. He stepped out, and found himself in an alley behind a building, in one of the four large habitats of Victory Station.

Vague light from the nearby star shone through the environmental dome, and gave the scene a wintery atmosphere. George straightened his coat and stepped out on the main road, then followed the crowds toward the main traffic hub.

People were beginning to assemble in long rows. Guards with guns and riot gear were positioned around the gates, and several people were dragged off to the side and interrogated. At the first opportunity, George moved off to one side and took another street towards a quiet alley. There he found a bar and sat down, keeping a watchful eye on the guard near the door. A Vidscreen on the wall came to life, displaying footage of the burning ships on the platform. Soldiers and fireman running, trying to contain the damage.

George chuckled quietly as he watched this distraction. A face then appeared on the screen.

His face.

He cursed under his breath. How had they managed to identify him? He had kept his helmet on the whole time he was on the ship. Below his face on the screen was a single word.

With a thud his glass hit the surface of the bar. "Traitor" it read in bold letters.

His fingers turned white as his hand clamped around the glass. How dare they call him that!

He was a war hero. He had wrestled this very station from the hands of the enemy, had in fact sacrificed everything for this rusted piece of space junk. A man standing at a podium came into view, and avoiceover started.

"James Miller, candidate for Governor, gave a speech moments ago, condemning the atrocious act committed at the docking bay today."

More footage followed showing several bodies, apparently mutilated by heavy gunfire. George's face darkened. He knew with absolute certainty, he had targeted two empty ships. His ship's scanners had confirmed only non-living cargo on them, and none of the bodies, they were showing had suffered the kind of damage his ships guns would have created.

This was the work of someone else; he was being set up.

"A terrorist by the name of George Harris created a bloodbath today. Known as the Butcher of Victory Station, the former general killed several innocent people, for reasons unknown."

The footage changed back to James Miller and his press conference. George's heart missed a few beats. Behind James stood a young girl flanked by two guards.

Anna.

That bastard bought his little girl. James Miller had set a trap, found the perfect bait, and George had walked right into it. Damn! With both fists, he hammered the bar in anger. He stopped and looked around.

The room grew eerily silent. People were staring from his face, up to the screen, and back. Slowly he stood up, threw a few credits on the bar, and reached for his bag. He felt their stares on him as he exited the building; he stayed in the shadows and hurried away before the soldiers or police arrived.

~

George reached for the small metal ridge, and held it while he leaned forward. He carefully placed his foot on the pitted metal surface. Below him was a dark, ice-cold abyss.

An ominous sounding breeze blew through this low oxygen area, and he had been crossing this gap for the last hour.

Just like home, he thought and grinned.

He took a laser from his belt and burned a hole in the wall, fastening a spike and attaching his rope to it. He waited a few seconds, then began repeating the procedure.

Slowly and methodically, he reached the other side and sat down. His fingers were all but frozen; his muscles hurt all over, but he made it.

He continued his voyage through small access corridors, some of which were barely large enough for a grown man to walk in. After walking crouched over for what felt like an eternity, he entered a larger open space with a sealed hatch on one side labeled "SECTOR 2" in stenciled letters. There was no lock.

From the access tunnel beyond it, he finally reached the innards of the central station dome and mingled with the crowd. It was dark and nobody paid much attention to him, or seemed to notice who he was. In the distance he could see the tall military headquarters. His headquarters, at one time. As he walked, the buildings around him changed, becoming less luxurious; most were lacking maintenance.

He stopped before an abandoned building, which clearly hadn't been used in many years. A faded nameplate hung askew on the door. George touched it briefly before he entered the house.

She used to live here, before he met her and took her as his wife. Such a pity her family wasn't as open to the invasion force as she was. They refused to see him the way she did. He sat down in a dusty chair and closed his eyes.

Outside, a shadow detached itself from a building down the block, binoculars trained on the house. The recon soldier touched his comm-pad. "Subject has entered the building, as predicted."

~

George opened his eyes, his hand already on his gun. Quickly, he leaned over in his chair, and rolled to the side as several figures poured into the room. He managed to fire two shots, and two men dropped to the floor. He tackled the third man before he could make it back through the door.

A short fight ensued before the last assailant lay on his back, pinned to the floor with a knife against his throat.

"Who sent you? Can't be the Governor, since you're clearly not military."

"I spit on the governor. But more than that, I spit on you, George Harris the Butcher!" The accent was unmistakable.

It reminded him of his wife. "Look, I don't want to hurt you, but they have my daughter. She is one of you. I need your help."

"I would never help you . . . I hate you! Death to the oppressors!"

George tied the man up and gagged him, then removed his weapons. He immobilized the other two. They should be thankful he was only using stun ordnance. Their protests however, suggested none of that.

George experienced a moment of blindness, as the room was bathed in light. Outside, police arrived and all of them had their weapons pointed at the house. "Come out with your hands up."

This house was supposed to be secret and inconspicuous, but George thought it was busier than a shopping mall during the holiday season. He sighed and grabbed his weapon.

~

The door swung open and police poured into the house. Quickly they split up to cover the kitchen and the living room, while a full squad climbed the stairs and searched the upper floor. There was no sign of George.

The commander of the squad had a slight tremor in his voice when he reported in. "No sign of the terrorist."

"Stand down commander. Let him go." The soldier looked at his comm-pad puzzled, but gave the order. It wasn't his place to question his superiors.

George slid the metal lid back on the manhole, and watched the activity at the house. How had they known he would be here? Who could have pointed this place out as a possible hideout? Only one person would know about it.

"They tortured her. The bastards will pay for this." He retrieved the comm-pad he had taken from one of his assailants, and connected to the grid. He wouldn't have long before they discovered it, but it might just be enough.

There it was: James Miller, and there was the address of his residence.

George stared at the picture. That piece of space-slime had not only taken his daughter, but he was keeping her in the same house she had lived in as a child, when she was still with him.

He flipped through the pictures, and halted at an image of a small courtyard; it was here she had done her first training. A smile appeared on his face.

~

James Miller's residence—the Commander's Residence in George's day—was situated in an elite area of Sector 2, close to the military headquarters and government buildings.

Two lonely police officers were lingering around the entrance. George passed by the house, watching the grounds, and as he passed them, he made his move. They were easily overwhelmed.

He dragged their unconscious bodies inside and closed the door. The code was exactly the same as it had been when this was his residence.

Inside he found a peculiar smell, confusing to his brain. Then he remembered—it was his wife's perfume.

Quietly he walked up the stairs towards the main floor which provided a brilliant view of the entire domed city. The main room was brightly lit, and a girl in a cocktail dress stood before the French doors, looking out on the balcony.

"Anna?"

She spun around. "Dad? Oh my God! How did you find me? The message, did you receive it? I can't believe it reached you!"

She fell into his arms. Her scent enveloped him; he had missed it for so long.

It would be all right. He knew what to do. There was a small military dock situated on the other side of sector two. It was only used by high ranking civilians and military. There would be limited protection; they could steal a ship and then—

A strong pain exploded in his abdomen. He felt strange. His legs stopped working and he fell to the ground. His hand found a knife, lodged in his stomach.

Military boots in large numbers approached from all sides. James Miller appeared; Anna moved to his side and put her arm around him.

George looked up in surprise. "Anna? Sweetie, I don't understand."

"Oh Daddy dear, isn't it obvious? I've always despised you, and when I was finally able to escape your military education, I ran away.

"A trader brought me back to where I belonged . . . where I found my husband. That wasn't enough though, don't you see? Your people are still controlling this station. With my husband's connections, I was given a position high within the police force. I sent you that note, then placed the traces in the brothel. You see, you had to be here, on Victory Station. With you branded as a terrorist, James will win the election, and we will control the station."

"But, why?"

"Because Dad, there is a fleet waiting to take this station the moment the main defenses go down. That is why. We will finally be liberated. Everything you did to us, to our people, everything you thought you accomplished in your entire life, will be for naught."

"Anna . . . you are my daughter; I love you. How could you do this to me?"

"Remember when you were the commander here? Remember when you used my mother to infiltrate the resistance, and then had her killed with the rest of them?"

"I had no choice. The mission had to succeed; I had to do it. We all made sacrifices. How did you find out?"

"Even kids have ears, Dad. I overheard you give the command. I cried so much, but I knew I couldn't show you my tears, or I might be next. Just like the time you killed my pet rabbit. The pattern was obvious, you are a heartless murderer."

"Honey, the rabbit was only to teach you about—"

"Be quiet old man! I will tell you what I learned. I learned that there was no choice for me, other than to be a good girl. I did all your horrendous training, I turned away all friendships because you did not want me to mingle with the locals. Not that it mattered . . . we never stayed long enough anyway. I used to cry myself to sleep every night. Only one thing kept me going—the knowledge that one day I would be able to avenge my mother, and save my people. That day is today. So now I must leave you on your new, and final, journey."

"How can you do this? This is horrendous. Thousands will die!"

"Oh Daddy, did you forget? Like father, like daughter." She bent down and grabbed his gun.

Two shots echoed through the room, before she turned and followed her husband down the stairs.

Always on the Outside

Michelle Murray

Always on the outside
Never fitting in
Always on the outside
Looking in
Always on the outside
Standing on the sidelines
Always on the outside
Never fitting in
Always on the outside
Wondering
When will it be my turn
For a smile or inside joke?
My turn to be inside the fence
Sliding into second base
Getting high fives, and raised up
On other's arms
Or will I always be
Standing on the outside
Never fitting in

The Collector

Phil Gladden

I was in a magical place, with warm breezes and sweet smells. Not like flowers, honey, fresh fruits, or anything I have ever known. A man-like creature came up to me. He was sweating, bleeding, cursing, and eating small cakes shaped like heartaches. Everywhere he went, he skipped rather than walked. He had a silly toothless grin and a nervous little insane laugh.

I asked him, "What is the reason for your visit on this fine sunny day?" As he thought about his answer, the sky grew dark and clouds rolled in.

He smiled and said, "I have come to make all your dreams come true."

"All of them?" I asked. "Even those which I speak of to no one? Even the dark, twisted dreams that lurk deep inside? The ones I hide, even from my own eyes?"

"Especially those," he said, as he began to drool.

"What is the cost? Nothing comes without a fee. Is it money you seek? as I have little. Is it my immortal soul? Sorry, but the devil tricked me out of that long ago, when I was young and foolish. What could I possibly use to pay for such a gift as answered dreams?"

He scratched his long-pointed chin, then looked at me as if sizing me up for a tasty meal. He spat on the ground causing the dust to stir, then paused for dramatic effect—or perhaps he was only lost in thought, and slow to speak.

"Give me all your memories, so I may explore the oceans and mountain tops you have seen. Give me the memories of your first kiss. The heated breath you shared with Judy Fulton, in the darkness of that summer night, on the dirt road off highway eighteen. I also want the one of the large-mouth bass you caught, with the fat worm you dug up from the compost pile at your grandfather's house."

He drew closer. His foul breath reeked as he made his demands. "I'll need the memory of your mother dropping you off at school, the first day of the first grade—the look of love mixed with nervous fear on her face as she waved, then turned, and walked away from the child, who until that day had been her constant companion, never more than a step and an arm's length away. I need *all* the memories you have of her ... especially of her."

As he spoke, his voice grew louder and the color ran from his face. "I want the ones from the time you hit the game-winning home run, that surprised all of the older children; including when they carried you off the field on their shoulders and made you feel like life had some sliver of hope.

"I want the memories of all the girls you knew growing up, and more importantly, the ones you dreamed of knowing. I want your little memories, too. From the red throats and stretched necks of the baby Robins you climbed the oak tree to see, to the cool sweetness of the ice cream you enjoyed, that came from the pink truck that played 'You Are My Sunshine.'

"I will need the memories of everything, and everyone, you ever loved. All of them I say . . . but I want the happy ones first. You may keep the sad ones, but only for a while."

I weighed his words, then as quickly as he had spoken them, the answer welled up from inside me, almost bursting to break free. "The price you ask is too high. Without the memories of all that I have loved, for what will I live? Even my darkest dreams could not fill that immense void, or give me purpose. Besides, if I gave up my memories, you would have all that I am. I fear you are not to be trusted. The price is too high," I yelled. "Be gone you evil, putrid spirit."

He reached into his pocket and removed his card. Across it, written in blood was his name. "They call me Alzheimer, and you have no say in this deal; for I take what I want, and time is always on my side."

He rode away laughing, on a bicycle made of bones, ash, and broken promises.

Tears rolled down my cheeks and formed pools on the ground. I sat and rested under the shade of a cottonwood tree until sleep overtook me.

I woke in a small room that smelled of bed sores, sweat, and urine. Young girls in tight skirts changed my diaper, and spoke to me as if I were a child.

Frivolous dreams rushed in, then disappeared carrying my priceless memories with them.

I sat and stared until the light faded into blindness, and death became a welcomed friend.

On the Fly

Sarah Henry

The fly makes its happy
rounds in my apartment.
Faster than a speeding cockroach,
it buzzes with excitement.
A fly is so dumb,
it can mate with
the speck from a pencil.

The fly makes its thrilled
rounds, landing on the TV
and other points of interest.
Then it brakes on the kitchen floor
and mates with a cockroach.
The cockroach is aroused
to dark passions.
They bond with each other
like two neighborhood bullies
and march toward me
in lockstep, shoulder to shoulder.

I reach for a flyswatter and
try to kill them with a gesture.
They run away and hide,
with the audacity of household
pests and the temerity of termites.

Echoes of Silence

Ed Ahern

Abbot Gregory watched Alan Carstairs shiver in his chair. It was November, and the dressed stone walls and slate floor of the office encouraged coldness.

"Mr. Carstairs, Brother Tobias has been away from the world for three years. Why would you be interested in him anymore?"

"Has he told you of his former occupation?"

"He confessed his past life before entering our order."

Carstairs half-smiled. "Then you can surmise why I'm here."

Gregory frowned, his forehead wrinkling up into his bald pate. "No, I can't. What is your purpose?"

"We need Tobias's special gift."

"Pardon?"

"Damage control for Homeland Security. We have a prisoner hiding critical secrets. Two of our best, using advanced techniques, were unable to get past his cover story. Toby is a maestro, a wizard of interrogation. Until he fell apart and got religion—no offense—he was our best at crawling inside a suspect's head and dragging out the truth."

Gregory pushed his chair back away from his desk, distancing him from Carstairs by several more inches. "We're recluses, not sadists."

"Father—"

"I'm a brother, not a priest."

"Brother Gregory. It would be a brief assignment. We'd pick him up, and bring him back in three days, four tops. We would pay the monastery seventy-five thousand dollars, which I believe could be put to urgent use."

Gregory stood up and half-turned his back to Carstairs. "Use your own people."

"Our best already failed. Toby's current innocence might even help him to better extract the information."

"An innocent torturer is a contradiction in terms."

Carstairs compressed his lips. "The additional questioning will take place with or without him, but Toby's expertise would ease its severity. May I talk with him before I leave? In your presence of course . . . and please, be sure to tell him it involves Brian."

Carstairs glanced around at the shelves, loaded with old books. His expression showed distaste, as if he suspected paper lice and bookworms.

Gregory observed the expression. "It is only proper that I tell him of your visit. Please wait here, and feel free to look through any of the books on the shelves." The Abbot retrieved his cane and shuffled out of the office. Fifteen minutes later Gregory returned with a tonsured monk.

"Hello Toby," Carstairs said. "You've lost weight. Wish I could." Tobias nodded to Carstairs but said nothing.

Gregory waved Tobias toward a chair, and turned to Carstairs. "Brother Tobias is under a discipline of silence. If he requests it, I will allow a dispensation to speak."

Carstairs' smile was tense. "Toby, I hope your recuperation is going well. It's the Brian situation. We finally trapped the bastard, but interrogators two and four—you know how good they are—were unable to break him. You also know how desperately we need what's locked in his head. We'll give you six month's pay for four days' work, in addition to what I promised the abbot. You can donate it if you like. Please, Toby; we're desperate. I'm desperate. We'll do whatever you need."

Brother Tobias had been staring at Carstairs with cat eyes. Several seconds later,, Tobias put his finger tips to his lips, then pointed at Abbot Gregory.

"You are granted permission to speak, Brother Tobias."

Tobias cleared his throat twice. "It's Tobias now, not Toby. The job shattered me, Alan, and I'm done with it. You already know my methods."

"We had to stop trying to duplicate your procedures, Toby. Sorry . . . Tobias. We couldn't keep the mix right, too many negative consequences."

Tobias flinched. He'd left because he couldn't stand those consequences.

Carstairs continued, "You know his story; Brian's a perp, not some harmless victim. We need your potions and that uncanny ability of yours."

Tobias glanced at Gregory. The Abbot's expression was impassive, but Tobias knew they desperately needed the money to keep the monastery afloat. He looked back at Carstairs, who also showed no emotion. *A room full of poker pros and I'm the mark. But it IS about Brian.*

"If I were to agree and crack him, you'll agree to release him with fresh documentation, no gimmicks."

Carstairs paused. "If it eases your conscience we could release him after we verify his information. He'd be a spent cartridge at that point."

"All terms in writing, witnessed, including his release if I get results. And a guarantee that this is the last thing you'll ask."

"You know we don't allow any paper trails . . ."

"In writing, or no deal."

"Jesus. Abbot, would we have your blessing to use Toby, ah, Tobias as we've discussed?"

Abbot Gregory had the annoyed look of a hockey fan who'd lost track of the puck. "I will need to talk to my superiors. If Brother Tobias is willing, and if I receive permission, then I won't object."

"Thank you both. Abbot, the monastery's Gregorian chants are truly inspirational; it's good to know that the singing will continue."

Brother Tobias ushered Carstairs out and returned to Gregory's office. The Abbot's bony frame had sunk back into his chair. "Carstairs is quite the oily functionary."

Tobias nodded agreement.

"Your task is odious, like flushing out latrines, but patriotism aside, your service would provide the monastery with power and heat for months. I regret your being immersed in this spiritual cesspool, but your faith should save you from being soiled by it."

Tobias stood in silence. Gregory, in his ignorance, was wrong; Tobias knew what he would need to do, and God wouldn't be taking part. *The wages of sin are generous. I wonder if they can be atoned for.*

~

Brother Tobias waited under the arched entryway to the monastery, listening for the sounds of an approaching automobile and staring at the stubbled corn fields across the road. It was just above freezing and the sodden wind blew through his wool robe as if it were gauze. His hands began to ache, and he put down his small overnight bag to rub them together.

He'd packed one change of underwear and sandal socks, planning on hand washing the day's linens each evening. Even with a breviary and small wooden cross in the bag, there was room to spare.

Poverty has its advantages.

A gray SUV arrived. The driver had a slight Hispanic accent, and his heavy holster made his sport coat bulge. The only words he spoke during the forty-minute drive were "Seatbelt, please," but even this was edged out by Tobias' complete silence. The ride ended at a brick office building, adorned with barred windows and painted-over glass. Tobias pushed the buzzer next to the faux-wood metal door and waited.

"Identify yourself."

Tobias said nothing but turned his face toward the security camera mounted above the door.

"Identify yourself! Oh, the monk. Wait a second, while I contact your escort."

Less than a minute later the door buzzed, swung back a few inches, then was pulled completely open by another bulging sport coat, who studied him while holding a picture.

"Brother Tobias? I understand you don't talk. Come with me."

Inside the door was a security station, complete with metal detector and conveyer-belted x-ray machine. Once frisked and scanned, Tobias was escorted to Carstairs' office. The massive wood desk suggested seniority, if not authority.

"Please sit down, Toby. I'll take you to your room when we're finished. The cafeteria is closed, but I can get someone to raid the refrigerator, if you're hungry."

Tobias shook his head no. He used his palm and index finger to indicate writing.

"Of course, here's an electronic tablet. I can read what you write on my computer and phone."

Tobias fired up the machine and began to type. 'Will stay mute, except for questioning Brian. You have drugs I asked for?'

"Of course. The first interrogation is scheduled for 8:30 tomorrow morning. The polygraph equipment is already set up. What else do you need?"

'Just caffeine & coke shot pre-polygraph. If he beats machine, need go to delusion and pain procedures. Need to check out machine this eve.'

"No problem." Carstairs looked up from his computer screen. "You know how sorry I am about that thing four years ago. We screwed up; but if this goes well I think I can get you back on the team . . ."

'No chance,' Tobias tapped. 'You know he'll be damaged goods by time I'm done?'

"Can't be helped. Follow me to the exam room."

Tobias spent twenty minutes checking settings and attachments on the lie detector and preparing the morning dosages, before Carstairs led him up to a small bedroom.

"I'm sorry, Tobias, but we're going to be locking you in for the night. The door unlocks at six tomorrow morning."

~

Tobias was normally asleep by 9:00, but the warm room and soft bed made him as restless as his thoughts. *Can I justify doing Judgement Day on him? Can I stay spiritually fit if I do this? Maybe . . . and not a chance.*

He washed his underwear in the bathroom sink and draped it over a radiator to dry. Then he prayed, first for Brian, then for his fellow brothers, and lastly for himself. His final conscious thought was of the clock in his room reaching toward one a.m.

The next morning Tobias ate while sitting near, but not among, the interrogators and guards. He recognized several of them, but knew they'd been instructed not to fraternize with him.

A uniformed guard approached as Tobias was finishing off some leather-skinned scrambled eggs. "Brother Tobias? Come with me please."

Brian was already in the examination room, cuffed to his chair and fitted with polygraph sensors. He was dressed in scrubs and his hair was unkempt and greasy; his body had the almost universal pudge of a man in his forties.

"Hello, agent Toby."

Tobias cleared his throat. "Hello Brian. Here's what's going to happen. You'll be questioned using techniques and drugs you're not trained to counter. If I don't believe what you say during the first session, I'll use more painful drugs and techniques. I'll be wired into you: pulse, respiration, brain activity. I'll feel your pain . . . and sense your lies."

"You idiots will call me a liar, even when you can't prove it. What's the point of abusing me?"

Tobias ignored the comment. "Here's the rules. If you refuse to answer, or garble, or prattle nonsense, you'll be electroshocked. Like this."

Tobias pushed a button, and Brian's body convulsed, his head snapping back and forth.

"Hurts like hell, doesn't it? Avoid the pain, answer the questions."

Brian shrugged off the residual pain and glared at him.

Tobias admired his tenacity. *It's good to be set against a professional; more satisfying.* Then guilt rushed over him. *Have I already turned back into Torquemada?*

"Be as still as you can while I set up this injection, otherwise you'll bleed. It's a metered flow, you'll be on drugs throughout. I'm shooting you up with caffeine and cocaine. You'll think you're having a heart attack. You're aren't . . . quite."

Brian's look was pressurized hate waiting to burst loose. "What's with the funeral dress, Toby boy?"

"It's Tobias now. Until yesterday I was a monk, growing vegetables."

"Well, my pious farmer, when I get out of here I'll make arrangements about you."

Healthy attitude. Tobias signaled to an assistant who wired and pressure cuffed him so he could viscerally sense Brian's reactions.

Tobias checked the monitors. The drugs had Brian trembling. They would distort his responses, but would also make it difficult for him to maintain his anti-interrogation training.

"Let's begin. Please state your name."

"Brian Peabody, you cretin."

Tobias briefly shocked him. "No editorial content, please. Where do you live?"

As the preliminary questions droned on, Tobias could feel the man tensing. *He's done this several times before, knows the trap questions will come in the middle of the easy ones, like the rare raisins provided in our monastery oatmeal.*

"Have you ever revealed classified information?"

Brian paused to stabilize himself. "No."

Even in his agitated state, Tobias sensed only faint quivers in the machine readings. *He's good.* But small shadings, a slight change of expression, a shift in the focus, an inflection in tone, told him that the answer wasn't truthful. Tobias had broken Russian agents trained to beat polygraph examinations, but he sensed Brian was even better. *Hopefully these drugs are enough.*

As the questioning continued Tobias grudgingly admired Brian's Zen-like composure. *I'm interrogating you by a book you've already read. Where are you in there?*

Tobias adjusted the drug inflow as the interrogation continued, an hour of questioning followed by a thirty-minute break to discuss the results with Carstairs, then more interrogation, break, and finishing after the third hour of questioning. Brian had begun to sweat after the first fifteen minutes, and Tobias felt the readings get less precise as the skin contacts moistened.

Despite the drugs, Brian beat the machine—but not Tobias. He leaned in as their machine hook ups were being disconnected. "Brian, I have to congratulate you. That was very, very good. Too good in fact. We both know the questions you fudged. Tomorrow we'll try a different approach. It has serious side effects that I'd like to spare you."

"I didn't think you cared. Do your worst. You can't hang me for what I don't admit to."

Tobias sighed. "Brian, as God is my witness, I don't want to ruin your mind. You have no reason to trust me, and I appear to have every reason to lie, but there's a way for you to get out of here uninjured. If you agree to get back on that machine and tell me the truth I'll spare you mental violation. Even better, you'll leave this facility without being arrested. Jobless, homeless, but free."

Brian's stare was stony. "Your horror movie robe doesn't scare me."

"You did what your case officer asked. They've had several months to use the information. Surely they'd understand if you protected yourself? Your future usefulness to them is nil. Please, Brian, save yourself."

His expression softened. "Nice try. We both seem to be locked into our roles."

"Just think about it. Meanwhile, I'll arrange for you to take a shower. Supervised, of course."

Brian laughed. "Please. It's way too late for Good Cop."

Carstairs was waiting for Tobias outside the examination room, his expression sour. "He didn't tell you anything."

Tobias began tapping on his tablet. 'Told me everything I need. Know where he lied, that's where he gave away secrets. You have chems for tomorrow?'

"Yeah. Scopolamine, sodium thiopental and midazolam. Quite the witch's brew."

On the walk back to his room Tobias silently recited his Vespers prayer, and by the time he sat on his bed his sense of composure had almost re-emerged from hiding.

He prayed, this time for himself, thinking that he needed it most.

~

The procedure resumed the next morning. Brian had cleaned up nicely.

Tobias paused before giving him the injection. "Brian, listen to me while you're lucid. These drugs are going to badly disorient you. They're not perfect. There is no real truth serum, but you'll become pliant and suggestible. They're also dangerous, a negative reaction could spark a brush fire burning up some of your brain cells. You don't have to take the risk, just tell me what we need to know."

"Sounds like a guilty conscience, Tobias. Let's get on with it."

He administered the drugs and studied Brian as they were being hooked up together. *He's screwed. Even if we let him go, his former team will interrogate him yet again. No wonder he's stoic.*

As the drugs took hold, Brian's pulse and breathing were like his slurred words, erratic and halting. He laughed at unfunny questions and Tobias sensed him involuntarily wetting himself.

"Have you provided information to a person or organization for money??"

"Naw, hell no. Have to be stupid to do that."

"Are you in the employ of a foreign government?"

"Nah. Working for one government is hard enough."

Tobias led him through a tangled chain of questions his deranged mind couldn't keep track of, zapping him when he wandered off the path. As his thinking shattered, Brian began revealing things.

"You said your contact's name was Ballitnikov . . ."

"Wrong again. It's Volodka, honest too, not like you."

"You told Volodka about the agent code named Celery."

"Celery, Asparagus, you'da thought we were Vegans."

Through the broken filters of his conscious mind, Brian began to sense Tobias' emotions through the two-way loops that connected them—his cringing shame at the intrusion and fears for both of them. Brian tried to push him out, but fumbled like a drunk warding off blows.

After fifty-five minutes he reacted badly to the drugs, convulsing and shaking the equipment so violently that accurate readings were impossible.

Tobias picked up his tablet and typed. 'Have to stop or he short circuit. Give him shot to counteract drugs. Need to flush out system.'

Carstairs came on the intercom while Brian was being strapped onto a litter.

"We didn't get everything we need. You have to repeat the process."

Tobias glanced over at Brian, who was still writhing, even after a second shot. He tapped out, 'Can't. Would kill him before I extract info. No choice, we go tertiary.'

"You up for it?"

'Never.'

Tobias had tried to hide in his mind during the worst of the second procedure, visualizing himself in the monastery's wainscoted chapel during devotions, trying to react to Brian's anguish and dementia as if they were Latin chants. He'd failed; the somatic reactions had surged through Tobias's system, and as Brian gave his befuddled accountings, Tobias could taste the shame and fear for giving so much away.

It hadn't been enough, though; Brian would suffer worse tomorrow morning.

I abandon a vow of silence so I can sin. Worse, I deform Brian's mind for dubious greater good. And God help me, I will do it again.

Tobias forced himself to eat a large supper, and to go to bed at his usual hour. *It was cleaner back when the accused were dunked underwater and condemned if they floated.* He had a brief, unkind thought about Brother Gregory and banished it, falling asleep just before 10 p.m.

~

When Tobias saw Brian the next morning he was trembling, his eyes half-empty of intelligence. He walked over and put his fingertips on the prisoner's forearm, leaning over to whisper, "Brian, try hard to listen to me. I'm offering the same thing as yesterday. Tell me everything and you walk. Don't tell and we go immediately to your third shot, a mixture of mostly cyclosporine and pravastatin. The drugs react with your system to create pain in every muscle. We then manipulate your arms and legs, producing greater agony without inflicting permanent damage or bruising. It's like a terrible attack of gout, but instead of just your feet or joints, it's all over your body. It's elegantly terrible; please don't force me to do this."

Brian's head had been bobbing while he spoke. "Nice guilt ploy. You got some of it, punk monk, but you'll never learn the rest. I can handle pain."

Tobias sighed. *He's already half fried. He won't make it. The pain will shred him.* "Let's begin."

Three minutes after getting the shot, Brian began shuddering, matted hair flopping across his forehead, eyes bloodshot and vacant. The questioning resumed. Brian's voice was guttural, as if his lungs hurt to speak. Every time he lied or denied Tobias would nod and a white-uniformed man would grasp one of his arms or legs and twist it. Tobias winced in sympathetic pain with each twist.

Brian's screams degenerated into gurgling moans, his eyes and nose began to run freely, and thick drool formed in the corners of his mouth.

Tobias had turned his head away but couldn't block Brian's pain inputs. He forced himself to stare. His pulse and blood pressure were chaos, and he knew Brian would shortly be going into a catatonic state. He nodded to the white uniform.

"Wait!" Brian screamed. "Wait."

Tobias waved off the orderly, stood up, still attached to cuffs and sensors, and leaned over so their faces were a few inches apart. "Brian," he whispered, "you're fighting to stay in a rat trap. Focus on the me that you feel. There's a way for you to escape both us and the Russians, but you have to give me the information first. Blink twice if you agree."

Brian blinked, then again. Tobias picked up his tablet. 'Alan, he's going catatonic. I'm giving him something to lower the pain.'

The response was quick. 'Bad Call.'

'Mine to make.'

Tobias put down the tablet, removed a vial from a refrigerator shelf, loaded a syringe and injected Brian, who passed out seconds later. Tobias sat back down in the chair next to him, waited several minutes, then woke Brian by gently wiping the tears and mucus off his face. He leaned over until his lips were against Brian's ear and began to whisper.

"I've given you the complete antidote, but please don't let it show. Listen to me; don't trust the identity they'll give you, you'll always be traceable, and at some point they may horse trade you for a spook of our own. Memorize this number: 203 222 1435. 203 222 1435. Call it from a burner phone. You remember the number?"

Brian blinked twice again, as Carstairs came onto the intercom. "Toby, what the hell are you telling him? Tell me now!"

Tobias ignored him. "Shall we resume, Brian?"

"Where did you usually meet Volodka?"

"Did you provide all of the Korean wartime contingency plan, or just certain chapters?"

"Which ones?"

Brian said he'd forgotten some information, and Tobias read him as truthful.

Tobias began typing on the tablet. 'That's everything significant, Alan. I'm finishing up.'

Carstairs lumbered into the room while Tobias was still standing in front of Brian, who silently mouthed 'Thank You.' Tobias smiled and mouthed back, 'You're Welcome.'

Carstairs was in his face. "Toby, what the hell did you just do?"

Tobias spoke out loud as he was stripping off the contacts. "Relax, Alan. You got the information, and it's legit. Now come through on your promise. And give me the info on his new identity, so I can check and make sure he's all right. You know what happens otherwise."

Carstairs subsided. "Yeah, we got a lot more than I thought we would. Once we verify a few things I'll release payment to you and the monastery. And I'll get the perp released with his new ID. It's what we agreed, but I don't like the way you just played me. What did you tell him?"

"Simple reassurances to gain his trust. Making it secret just made it more powerful. I lied, it worked; you got what you needed."

"See? Now that's the devious son-of-a-bitch I love. Come back with us, Toby."

"Never. Sorry. I'll clean up and get ready to go. And return to silence."

~

Abbot Gregory looked down at the two stacked piles of hundred-dollar bills on his desk, then up at Brother Tobias. "We're solvent for another year. I can look at you and guess what you had to undergo. You have our respect and thanks." He paused. "Ah, Brother Tobias, you're also under a vow of poverty, might we be able to utilize your six months pay as well?"

Tobias put his fingers to his lips, then pointed his hand at Gregory.

"Permission to speak."

Tobias cleared his throat. "Unfortunately no, Abbot. The money is committed to another charity."

"Do I know it?"

"No. It's quite small, and given to secrecy. With your permission, I'll take the money and go."

"Irregular, Brother Tobias, but very well, so long as you don't keep it."

That Sunday, Tobias joined the other monks in their chants. One hundred fifty people sat on hard folding chairs listening to them. When the performance was over the monks dispersed and the crowd began filing out.

Tobias met a man in an alcove and handed over a parcel.

"Not my business, Brother, but why does this guy get new docs and the deluxe treatment?"

"Sin offering . . . or maybe atonement for shared memories."

"What?"

"Never mind. Pox Vobiscum."

Corridors of the Mind

Nerisha Kemraj

The walls are closing in,
I feel it deep within
So many doors to take,
but which one seals my fate?

Noises erupt from inside-
laughter, while I cower,
trying to hide

So many choices
but not one true home
So many faces,
yet not one I know

These all lead to the same place
How do I escape?
Darkness looms over me
I'm not where I want to be.

The Muse

Kimberly Garrett Brown

He called her his muse.

Whenever she stood nude on the platform in the center of his studio, her body pulsed with anticipation. His work made her feel relevant.

But lately things were different. The lights that illuminated parts of her body and created hollows in others seemed to shine in the hidden creases of her mind. *What did it mean to be someone's muse? Was she stirring him to greater artistic heights? Or was she a way to help him forget his troubles and lessen his pain?*

The muses, the nine daughters of Zeus and Mnemosyne, did both. Though generally believed to be a source of inspiration to humans, she remembered from school that they had actually been created to commemorate the victory of the Olympian Gods over the Titans, and to help the Gods forget the sorrows of the past.

She took off her silk robe and draped it over the arm of the wooden bench next to his desk. He glanced her way but said nothing. She found her place on the platform and began to move through various poses as he sketched on a giant pad.

"Reclining today," he said as he turned to the easel.

She positioned herself among the pillows on the platform. The scratching whine of the saxophone, blaring from the speaker on his desk, made her skin crawl; she tried to ignore it.

He grunted.

She wondered if his apparent dissatisfaction was with his work or her body. Her stomach folded over the top of her pubic hair, hiding the majority of the perfectly trimmed triangle she'd started to maintain. Her once-tight breasts sagged like over-sized avocados, fighting to be as far away from one another as possible. She knew other women her age who had strict regimens of Pilates and Yoga to keep things tight and young-looking. But planks and up-dogs would never hide three pregnancies and an overdeveloped affection for wine and chocolate.

She struggled to focus. *How significant was the model to the artist?* She could be easily replaced by a younger, thinner woman; instead he chose her.

The way they had met was like a Lifetime movie. The kids were with their father for the weekend, and she had gone to a Friday night art festival at the museum.

She wasn't particularly interested in art but enjoyed the music and cocktails without the pick-up scene of a bar—though secretly she hoped she'd meet someone.

She walked through the exhibits at the museum, because it felt wrong not to at least look at the art. The random colors smeared across canvas reminded her of the paintings her kids had brought home as preschoolers.

She decided to get a drink and people watch. She ordered the Golden Goddess, named after the featured exhibit, but returned it after one sip. "I hate to be a pain in the ass, but this isn't working for me," she had said as she slid her drink across the bar toward the bartender.

"Not a fan of bourbon?" the bartender asked.

"Too sweet. Angel's Envy on the rocks."

"I love a woman who knows her bourbon," a man commented from behind her.

She feigned a smile and walked away.

There had been nowhere to sit. Groups of friends congregated around tables. Couples sat nestled together on benches. Families sprawled across blankets on the lawn.

Knee deep in people but utterly alone. She settled at an empty table. *What had she expected?*

Engaging strangers in conversation didn't create connectedness; it only made her feel more alone. But lounging on her sofa and talking to the television wasn't any better. The isolation made her anxious and depressed.

Since the divorce, and honestly for most of her marriage, she longed for that one person who was *her* person. Someone who couldn't wait to spend time with her. A true companion. A ride or die friend. Someone to go places with or just plain talk to.

"Mind if I join you?" he had asked, interrupting her thoughts.

"Sure," she said moving her purse off the chair next to her.

"I always come to these things hoping they'll be different," he said.

"They never are."

"And I don't know whether I should be flattered or insulted that they named such a girlie drink after my painting."

The Golden Goddess exhibit—a departure from the museum's contemporary slant—exuded sexuality and sadness in equal measures. It felt almost as if the viewer had intruded on that moment right after sex, when desire is spent and insecurities lay exposed. It was unclear whether or not the artist loved the women or their vulnerability, but she didn't share any of that as they talked about his paintings. Their conversation moved from art to culture, and then to food, making them both realize how hungry they were. They had walked to a local restaurant for dinner.

He invited her back to his studio, where instead of taking her to his bed, he drew her in charcoal. When he was done, she slipped on the robe he had given her, trying to look calmer than she felt. What if his drawing was like one of those horrible pictures her well-meaning friends always took, where her stomach was sticking out too far or it looked as if she had three boobs? The thought had nauseated her, but as she stood in front of the charcoal drawing, it felt as if she was seeing herself for the first time.

He stood behind her caressing the side of her neck with his lips; he wrapped his arms around her and untied the robe. He traced the curves of her body with his charcoal fingers. The robe slid to the floor. He knelt in front of her, kissing the inside of her thigh.

She stared at his drawing. He had seen beyond her facade of nonchalance and confidence, had captured both her vulnerability and her desire. That night she felt as if he had truly seen her.

She wasn't as sure now.

"You're creasing your forehead," he said.

Here and now. She slowly inhaled.

Their conversations never strayed far from his art. He'd casually mention his other models, but never by name only by medium. He described the hardiness of one woman as the permanence of oil, long-lasting but needing years to fully cure. Another he talked of the softness of watercolor.

When she asked why he drew her in charcoal, he'd pulled her close. "Your depth can only be captured in shades of gray."

She didn't know if that was good or bad. Nor was it clear if he drew from a place of affection or obsession. *Was he looking for affirmation or absolution?*

"You're frowning," he said, meeting her eyes for the first time that night.

She counted to five as she inhaled. *Here and now.*

They had been seeing each other—if you could call it that—for several months. They rarely went out. Never interacted with his friends or hers. Their evenings consisted of her posing, him drawing, and sex on the studio floor—mutually beneficial, but not real a relationship. It would never be more than what it was.

She had vowed this would be the last time, but being with him in this place, here and now, made her forget her sorrow. He was in fact, her muse.

The Ugly Side of Love

Nerisha Kemraj

So many years of memories,
all bursting with love.
But that too, has become...
a memory in itself.

Now, time holds
painful anniversaries,
and the remembrance thereof...
maybe the time has come
to empty out that shelf.

Love became the enemy,
replaced by disgust.
Still, we cannot forget the love,
or erase all of the past.

Experience makes fools wise.
It gives us much to think of;
a lesson to be learned,
where moving on, is a must.

Detective Drake

Adam Johnson

It was a perfect summer day in lower Chicago, that is until Detective David Drake received a call that would make his cold blood run colder. It was a day like any other. Detective Drake buttoned his white dress shirt and checked his equipment. He was still getting used to the new uniform. He had spent several years as a beat cop and finally made Detective a few months ago.

He put on his Chicago Bears hat, covering the small horns on his head; everyone knew what he was, but he felt like the hat made people more comfortable. Beaming with pride, he holstered his gun and walked out the door. It was time to pick up his new partner.

Drake opened the door to a beautiful black Dodge Challenger and hopped in, wiping some dust from the dash, and checking his broad pointed teeth in the mirror before peeling off.

He pulled into the drive of an upscale housing commons and double-checked the address on his phone. *This is it. Nice place.*

A slender man with olive skin and dark slicked back hair approached his car, holding a travel mug. Drake stepped out. "You must be Cortez. I'm Detective David Drake. Heard a lot about you, kid."

Cortez reached out and shook Drake's scaled hand. "Pleasure to be working with you, I know all about you as well." Cortez smiled, his bright white teeth almost glowing in the sunlight.

"Right." Drake peered at Cortez through the corner of his eye. "Well, let's get to it. Watch your feet getting in, and hold onto that coffee if you value your life," Drake warned. After a moment of tense silence, he said, "So, you were quite the hot shot on the beat, huh? I'm pretty impressed with how you took down that Moondust operation."

"Well, it wasn't just me. It was a coordinated effort." Cortez shot Drake a smile. The city was alive as they drove down the strip; people visiting stores, shopping, and stopping at their favorite coffee places. "You've had an impressive run as well, I hear. Top numbers in the academy, top numbers in arrests on the beat. It's a wonder they took so long to make you detective." He raised his coffee cup to his lips.

"That's nice kid, but you know how they feel about Dragonkin around here. My mother was a human, but they don't see that side of me. They just see the scales and the elongated pupils." Drake stared forward out the window. "Did you know, it's been thirty years since the last full blooded dragon was hunted and killed? My ancestors once policed the old laws; I actually come from a long line of cops. They may have been different, but they were brave and they upheld the law. You could say I was born to be a detective . . . but since my skin is different, it was a tougher road for me."

Drake's jaw moved to the side, and he clicked his tongue. "Enough about me, Rookie. Looks pretty quiet out here, how about we grab an early lunch? Chicago style deep dish, best in the world, my treat."

"Sounds great Drake, but let me pay half. I don't want to start out owing you." Cortez laughed and passed some cash to Drake.

"Good call, kid. I'll be right back." Drake disappeared into the Pizzeria and returned shortly carrying a huge box with steam escaping from its sides. They continued talking while they ate. Drake was mildly surprised with how well it was going. For months, every Detective in the Department had refused to work with him.

Cortez dabbed his face with a napkin. "You were right." He laughed. "That was the best pizza I've ever had. Smoke?" He produced a small pack from his pocket, and shook one loose for Drake. The hulking detective reached forward with a yellowish scaled hand, and took the cigarette between fingers with short talon-like fingernails.

"Dispatch to Drake. Over." A shrill voice came from the radio in the dash of the Challenger. "Drake, do you copy? Over." Drake grabbed the mic. "This is Drake, what is it, Dispatch? I'm on my lunch," he said, and exhaled a cloud of smoke.

"We've received several reports of black fire at the Crooked Tree in Fairy-Town. Go check it out and report back. Over." The voice cuts out with a short burst of static.

Drake's bright amber eyes widened, but he sat still in his seat.

After staring forward for a few moments, he radioed back. "Repeat that, Dispatch."

"Black fire at the Crooked Tree; I was clear, Drake. I can call Edwards and Guthier if you two aren't up to it."

"No, we're on it." Drake grumbled and reholstered his radio. The Challenger roared through a U-turn and sped north, toward Fairy-Town.

"Black fire sounds like the demons," Drake said. "But what would they be doing in Fairy-Town?" He gripped the steering wheel with white-knuckle force.

He didn't frighten easily, and was more than capable of handling himself. He was, after all, the son of one of the last full-blooded dragons. Yet this call had him on the edge of his seat.

"Do you think it's a mob hit?" the tall slender man in his passenger seat asked. His black hair reflected the sun, as he passed Drake another cigarette.

"Doesn't make any sense," Drake muttered. "The crime families have kept to their own turf since magical creatures gained equal rights with humans. If you ask me, the Integration of Magical Creatures Act is the best thing humans have done for this planet." Drake pulled a lighter to the tip of his cigarette. "No offense, Cortez."

"None taken," Cortez said, slinking down and lighting his own cigarette. "The treaties the families agreed to after IMCA have kept things relatively quiet, but maybe someone had a score to settle. It's not unlike demons to go back on their word."

"No, This is risking too much. The demons wouldn't risk breaking the treaties unless there was something worth more than their lives." Drake exhaled a sweeping cloud of smoke and spun the wheel hard to the right. "You may be too young to remember," Drake said through gritted teeth, "But before IMCA and the treaties, the crime families were ruthless to each other. The fairies were some of the worst. The Perillins family began corrupting demon children, as contradictory as that sounds. They would kidnap young demons and erase their memories, then train them and send them back to slaughter their own families. The Perillins don't own the Crooked Tree though, so I'm not sure what we are about to walk into."

~

The black-on-black Challenger came to a screeching halt in front of an old building, covered in flowering vines. Like many of the buildings in Fairy-Town, it resembled a vertical garden. "Here we are."

Drake grunted as he got out of the car. "I don't see any demon fire," he said, scanning the building. The windows in the front were broken out, the door creaked with the wind, holding on by one hinge. "Can you smell that?" Drake asked as he stepped forward.

"I don't smell anything," Cortez said, knowing that Drake's sense of smell was far superior to his own. He grabbed the mic from the radio. "Dispatch, stay on alert, send a unit for backup. We're going in."

They moved slowly toward the broken door to the restaurant, drawing their weapons. Drake signaled Cortez to cover him as he entered, then took care to step quietly around badly scorched overturned tables. Cortez followed through the broken glass littering the floor, trying to walk softly and quietly. Small crackles whispered through the dining room as they advanced toward the kitchen.

Drake raised his fist and they both froze. "I saw something move in the kitchen," Drake said quietly. "A quick shadow; let's move."

The rookie's voice shook. "Do you think they are still here?"

"Only one way to find out." Drake reared back and kicked open the kitchen door. "Chicago PD! Come out with your hands up!" Drake's eyes darted around the dimly lit room.

Most of the lights had been broken out, leaving only a couple to flicker, blanketing the room in soft light. Pans lay on the grill; tongs and stirring spoons spread across the floor. A single pot sat on a lit burner, steam pouring from it.

"Spread out," Drake said. "Clear the room." His large half-dragon body was an imposing sight—even Cortez was a little scared of him, especially in the soft light.

"Drake, over here. I got something!" Cortez stood in front of a convection oven.

"Dammit." Drake shook his head and spit at the floor. The spit briefly sizzled on the ground with a small puff of smoke. "These poor bastards," he said, walking up to the oven. "Their bones were split, in order to fit them in this way. This took time and effort." Drake closed the oven door. "Head back outside and radio Dispatch to send a Medical Examiner; we have several dead fairies and possibly some demons inside."

Cortez nodded and slipped back out the kitchen door.

Drake turned and saw a slightly opened door at the end of a short hall in the back of the kitchen. Raising his weapon, he slowly advanced toward it, and quietly opened the door a crack. Beyond it he could see a dark stairwell, leading to a lower level. His half-dragon eyes could see well in the dim light, so he carefully descended the stairs.

He reached the bottom, and stepped carefully through what appeared to be a storage area. *This place is a mess. What were they looking for?* He moved through boxes of cups and linens, and approached a shelving unit laying on the ground with spices and herbs littered across the floor. The wall where it had stood, now had a large gaping hole, with scorched edges.

Drake moved forward and sniffed the air. He scanned the dark room and stepped through the opening. The smell of burnt flesh hung heavy in the air, and his eyes began to water.

"Dammit." He cursed out loud as he took in the scene. Blood covered the walls in every direction. Lifeless bodies dominated the room. He bent down to inspect one. Its porcelain skin was still warm.

Drake turned toward the desk in the back of the room and heard a loud crunch. He looked down to see a fairy's jaw crushed under his boot. He winced and moved forward. A fairy lay motionless over the desk, its hands covered in black blood. *Must've killed a demon.*

Drake used a baton to roll the fairy over. The jaw was indeed missing from its face, a dry tongue hung lazily from the head.

Money was spread all over the desk. Drake turned and looked around; there was money and white powder all over the room. Perplexed, he checked the shelves around the room. Seemingly priceless antiques adorned the shelves. Some were shattered to pieces, but most were still intact.

A single bullet casing lay among the wreckage. Drake grabbed his handkerchief and picked it up to examine it.

"Well, well, well. If it isn't Detective Fake." The familiar voice came through the opening at the end of the room. "Did you do all this?" A tall aging man stood on the other side of the wall; short greying hair covered his head and a bushy grey mustache sat atop his lip.

"I would watch my mouth if I were you, Edwards." Drake snarled and spit next to older detective's feet. As his spit sizzled and created a little smoke distraction, Drake carefully slipped the bullet casing into his back pocket.

"Still can't control that napalm in your mouth, can you?" Edwards chuckled as he stepped into the scene. "We heard dispatch order some backup for you, so we figured you probably needed some help from real detectives."

"Looks like a messy scene. Good thing we came to help." Another familiar voice came from beyond the hole in the wall.

"Guthier, glad to see you took time out of your busy schedule of harassing kids to come here." Drake sneered as the short bulbous man entered the room. "I have this under control; you two can leave the way you came in."

"And leave a filthy lizard like you alone in here? I don't think so." Edwards scoffed. "Your partner called for help, here we are." He sauntered through the wreckage. "I wouldn't be surprised if you did do this."

A thin smile curled across his face as he leaned in close to Drake. "The only reason you made detective is because the Chief has a soft spot for you."

"You got somethin' to say to me, Edwards?" Drake snarled, standing to his full height. "I'd love for you to push me today."

"Hey, how did you guys get here?" Cortez called from outside the wall. Drake turned to them and clicked his tongue.

"We were having lunch up the street when we heard the call for backup." Guthier said.

"This guy can't turn down lunch." Edwards chuckled, motioning to his partner.

"Yeah, right," said Cortez. "It's just, I didn't see anyone come through the front door. "Tension filled the room as he entered through the hole.

A sudden call of radio static broke the silence. "Dispatch to Edwards. Are you on the scene? Over."

Edwards locked eyes with Drake and pushed the mic on his radio. "On the scene now, awaiting a CSI team to lock it down," he said staring at Drake. "Detective Drake was already on the scene. He's just catching us up to speed now." Another thin smile appeared under his mustache. A muffled succession of footsteps echoed from outside the walls. "Hello?" A dainty voice called from the stockroom. "Ann Carlson with the Chicago Medical Examiner's office. Is anyone here?"

"Over here," called Drake, his eyes trained on Edwards. "Looks like the M.E. is here. Come on, Cortez, let's catch the CSI team up top, and brief them on what we found." Drake pushed past Edwards and Guthier, followed by Cortez.

The two made their way back through the scorched restaurant, taking care not to disturb any more of the scene.

A tall thin man, wearing dark Aviators glasses and a blue windbreaker labeled CHICAGO P.D. CSI met them outside. "Oh look, Drake's on the case.

"Honestly, Drake, I'm glad you're here. These creatures are from you neck of the woods. Maybe you can ask them to knock it off, so I can go see my wife for once."

A myriad of laughs burst out from the rest of the team.

"Save it, Francis," Drake snarled. "I found this bullet casing inside, the only one as far as I could tell." He pulled out the folded up handkerchief from his pocket and handed it to Francis. "fairies and demons don't use guns. Why don't you run that and get me the results, eh?"

Drake spit on the grass, and it instantly shriveled, blackened, and began to smoke. "Come on, Cortez. Let's pay a visit to the Perillins, see what they know about this." Drake opened the door to the Challenger, and turned to see

Cortez leaning in close to Francis's head. "Cortez, we gotta move. Those bodies were still warm and so is the trail!"

"I just need to make a quick call," he said, pulling his phone from his pocket.

"We go now, Cortez!"

"You got it, Drake!" He nodded his head at Francis, and jogged over to the car. "Let's hit it, partner," he said. He pulled up his phone and began punching furiously at the keys.

Drake threw the car in gear, and the engine roared as they pulled away from the crime scene. The city was still alive, dominated by neon lights as dusk set in. In Fairy-Town, neon was a staple for every building. Large banners hung over the streets, mostly proclaiming fairies' cultural beliefs. The fairies were a proud race and took no shame in claiming their ways were the only ways.

The buildings here were equally as impressive. fairies liked to treat their entire property as gardens, including brick and concrete buildings. Many of the buildings in Fairy-Town had plants growing on them whose petals glowed when it got dark. Driving the streets of Fairy-Town at night was a spectacle to behold, and one Drake secretly enjoyed. Beautiful bright colors, woven perfectly into the night sky, with glowing petals and pollen falling from the flowers every night, causing a shower of soft light to fill the streets.

"Put your phone away and focus," Drake snapped. "You want to tell me what that was about back there?" He spit out of his window.

"What do you mean?" Cortez responded, with a slightly higher pitch in his voice as he deposited his phone in his pocket.

"What were you talking to Francis about?" Drake shot his piercing amber eyes toward Cortez. "If we are going to be partners, I need to trust you. I don't mean trust you to get my dry cleaning back on time, I mean I need to trust you with my life, my well being, and especially information."

"I was just asking him if he could send me the results of his lab tests as well," Cortez said matter-of-factly. "You know, since you only asked him to send it to you, *partner*." He sank back in his seat and shook out a cigarette. "Smoke?"

"Yeah." He said pulling it to his lips, lit it, and sighed heavily. "Sorry. I'm used to the whole department being against me." He took a deep drag and unleashed a swirling cloud of thick grey smoke.

"Partnerships are a two way street, Drake. I'm going to have to trust you too." Cortez lights his own cigarette. "I know what you dealt with. Don't you think that they warned me about partnering with you? Told me to just stay with the other Humans?" Cortez pulls a piece of cold pizza from the back seat and helps himself to it.

Drake holds out a napkin without a word.

"Right, sorry." Cortez situated the napkin under the slice. "You're a good cop, Drake. I know I can learn a lot from you." He took a bite and continued. "Plus, it helps to have the biggest guy in the department on your team." He chuckled as he fought to get the words out through a mouthful of pizza.

"Thanks kid, We're here." They pulled up to a towering building; this one wasn't covered in vines and flowers, but had plants strategically placed across the expanse of it. The symmetry of the building was perfect, and the placement of the plants mirrored that. The upper half of the tower was solid grey concrete, while the base of the tower was constructed of solid white marble. A grand stairway lead to two colossal wooden doors. Two Pale skinned figures flanked either side of the doorway. They looked like photocopies of each other—slicked back white hair, wearing navy-blue business suits. Their electric blue eyes were almost haunting, set against their porcelain skin.

"Fairies," Drake uttered as he climbed out of the Challenger. "Murderous Criminals." He growled. "Follow my lead, Cortez. Stay close."

Drake led the way up to the pair, mustering his full height and producing his badge from his pocket. "Detective David Drake, Chicago P.D. This is my partner, Detective Vincent Cortez. We're here to see Perrin Perellin. We have a few questions for her."

"Ms. Perellin isn't accepting visitors," the fairy on the left answered in a smooth voice. "You will have to arrange an appointment with her secretary."

"I'm not askin'." Drake spit on a handrail and the metal began to sizzle. "Either you let us in, or we will have the full force of the Chicago P.D. here in minutes."

"Hmm . . . all that talk, without a warrant," the other fairy mused. His electric blue eyes darted from them back to his colleague, who gave him a slight tilt of his head.

"Fortunately, Ms. Perellin is feeling generous today. She is on the 53rd floor." The two fairy guards opened the wooden doors, and gestured them inside.

The lobby was like nothing either of them had ever seen. It was covered floor to ceiling in different tones of marble. Plants hang from impossible heights and on either end of the lobby, a small waterfall fell through the plants and into a small wading pool. A small river ran through the middle of the lobby, and an expansive semicircular bridge climbed from one side to the other.

The two detectives were met by four more fairies who looked eerily similar to the two outside the door. Drake's phone vibrated in his pocket; he checked the screen. FRANCIS.

"Hold on fellas. I need to take this," Drake said, and he walked over to one of the wading pools. "Drake here," He answered quietly.

"Drake, you were right. It definitely wasn't a fairy using a gun. The shell casing came from a Luger 9 millimeter." Drake turned to see the guards staring at him impatiently.

"So, it came from our department?"

"There's a good possibility. We are cross referencing discharge reports and ammunition assignments with the serial number from the casing now, to see if we can pinpoint who it belonged to. Until then, keep your guard up, Drake."

"Thanks for the tip. We are at the Perellin Building now. Keep this line active, I'm going to try to get a confession out of her." Drake blacked out the screen, leaving the call connected, and deposited the phone back in his pocket, before rejoining Cortez and the guards.

"Everything alright, Detective?" The fairy in front asked with a thin grin.

"Perfect. My mother just needs help moving." He forces a chuckle. "Shall we?" He asks, motioning toward the elevators.

"I hope you don't mind a security escort," said one of the pale-skinned men, with a soft smile. "It's standard for all of Ms. Perellin's visitors; the top floor is zoned for private use."

"Of course not, lead the way." Drake may have been two times their size, but he knew what they were capable of. He leaned in to Cortez. "I don't like this, it feels like a trap. Stay sharp."

Cortez nodded as they continued toward a set of towering golden doors. Drake reveled in the fact that his partner had not been this quiet since they met.

The ride up the elevator was less than pleasant.

Drake scanned the compartment. *Four guards. Fairies don't need guns because they wield powerful magic.* Drake silently counted the floors. *Thirty-Three, Thirty-Four, Thirty-Five. We can take them if we have to, I just hope Cortez lives up to his reputation. Forty-Four, Forty-Five, Forty-Six.* He turned and nodded at the guard to his left. *Not so much as a smile. This is going to be fun. Fifty-One, Fifty-Two, Fifty-Three.*

The elevator came to a stop with a pleasant chime. The guards motioned them forward as the doors slid open.

Two fairies, cloaked in black, passed by before Drake could step out. They were pushing a cart with an ornate chest secured to it. One of the guards grabbed Drake's shoulder and steered him to the right.

I have to know what's in that chest.

The hall they were led down was wide, and lined with artwork. Copper colored frames held paintings of fairies dressed in ceremonial robes. Drake knew it was a tradition for fairies of great importance; he could even identify a few. "These must be the heads of the Perillin family."

They approached two dark-wood doors, adorned with gorgeous soft metal twisting throughout. Drake dropped his lighter, causing the guards to look down.

"Cortez, NOW!" He spit in the face of the guard in front of him, and the fairy's face began sizzling.

As the guard screamed in agony, Drake ducked a punch coming in from behind him. He lunged forward connecting a powerful punch to another guard's jaw, and was rewarded with an audible crunch of bone. He reared back to deliver another punch, when he felt cold metal touch the back of his head.

"That's enough, Drake." The familiar voice stung his ears like fire. "I am impressed though. You move fast for a big lizard."

"We have been partners for one day, Cortez, and you already let me down."

"Don't feel bad Drake. It would have been longer, but you really are a good detective." Cortez motioned for the remaining fairy guards to open the doors. "Too bad, too. I was starting to like you." He pressed the barrel into the back of Drake's head. "Move."

"It was your bullet I found in the Crooked Tree, wasn't it?" Drake shook his head. "That's why you needed to talk to Francis! Was it him you were texting on the way here? Because he already called to tell me that the casing belonged in our department. It won't be long before they find out it was yours."

They walked into a massive room. The walls were constructed with beautiful woodwork, and they met the marble floor with elegance. Precious antiques were displayed on pedestals along both sides of the room. At the head of the room sat a commanding wooden desk, decorated with expertly crafted carvings of fairies and their struggles. Behind it, a wall of glass overlooked Fairy-Town.

At the desk sat a slender fairy woman, with long flowing golden hair and perfectly smooth pale skin.

"No matter," said Cortez. "I will Just tell them you stole my weapon and used it to frame me. Who are they going to believe? Me, the star rookie, or you, the dirty lizard?"

"Is this true, Vincent?" a soft whimsical voice asked.

"Uh . . . y-yes ma'am. But it will be fine . . . they will believe me." Cortez tried to muster some confidence in his voice.

"That's too bad, Vincent. You showed a lot of promise." Ms. Perellin spoke softly.

"Wait! I can fix it . . . just hold on a—"

Ms. Perellin flicked her hand, and two fairies grabbed Cortez by the arms and began to drag him.

A gunshot rang out, followed by a pronounced thud. Ivory hair lay spread across the ground and a single hole now sat between the dead guard's eyes.

Cortez started to turn his gun on the other, but was met with a jet of black flame. The smell of burning hair and flesh filled the room almost as quickly as his screams.

Drake snarled and turned his attention back to Ms. Perellin. "So, it wasn't demons at the Crooked Tree. It was you! Killing your own people!" Drake spit on the floor, burning a hole in what he assumed to be an expensive rug. The three remaining guards lined up at the door behind him.

"It was simply business, Detective. I run Fairy-Town, and they kept a secret from me. No one keeps secrets from me." Her electric blue eyes flared, resembling crackling blue flames. "However, in the interest of business, I couldn't just send my people in. That would have sent a powerful message, but fairies are a proud race; if the whole of Fairy-Town knew that we slaughtered them and destroyed a fairy business, there likely would have been revolts. I am too close to ultimate power, to risk that." She smiled softly and motioned to her guards. "So, we learned to conjure black flame. After all, fairies have always had a poor relationship with demons."

"What was it you were looking for?" Drake scanned the room. "It was in that chest wasn't it?"

"On your knees, Detective." Ms. Perillin ordered. Two of the guards approached and placed their hands on each of his shoulders.

"Tell me what it was!" Drake demanded.

One of the guards kicked the back of his knees, forcing him to the ground.

"Don't act like you couldn't feel it, Detective." Ms. Perillin said, as she rounded her wooden desk. "Everyone knows that dragonkin can sense their own kind." A dark smile crossed her face, and she tilted her head down, looking Drake in the eyes. "There was one dragon egg that survived The Hunt, and it was being held at the Crooked

Tree. These humans think they know what's best for us. They killed your entire family, they treat you like less than a house pet, and yet you still defend them!" She paced in front of her desk. "I will raise the dragon as my own, and use it to bring the humans to their knees, just like your are now."

Gunshots rang out from the hallway, followed by piercing screams. Her eyes lit up as she lifted her hands. Black smoke began to rise from them as flame danced across her fingertips.

Drake swept the legs from under the guard to his right. As the fairy crashed to the ground, Drake jumped behind the guard on his left, feeling the scorch of black flame run past his arm.

He charged Ms. Perellin, gripping the guard's suit and using him as a shield. Black flame climbed around the fairy guard, and the sound of crackling flesh filled Drake's ears. He pushed the charred guard toward her, and she casually batted him to the side.

Drake saw his opening and tackled her to the ground, pinning her wrists to the floor.

The wooden doors burst open. "Chicago P.D. Don't move Perellin, it's over!"

"My time will never be over!" she screamed, as she bucked and managed to roll Drake off of her. Crouched on the floor, she raised her hands toward Drake as black flame began to slither around her fingers, the fire in her eyes matching the intensity of the flame.

Drake threw his arms over his face, and a single gunshot filled the room. He heard a thud hit the floor and peered through his arms.

Ms. Perellin lay lifeless on the floor, her golden hair perfectly draped over her body. He stood up and saw a bullet wound in the center of her forehead.

"That was a close one, huh?" the Chief said as he approached Drake. He was a tall, stocky man, with a bald head, just like Drake's. "Francis told us what was happening. We listened in, and as soon as we heard you start fighting, I dispatched the SWAT team, and well . . ." The large man smiled. "I had to see this one for myself."

"Sir, there is a lot I need to fill you in on." Drake was relieved it was the chief who showed up.

"Tell me over dinner. It's been a long night." He put his arm around Drake, and they walked toward the doors. "Deep-dish, right?"

"Best in the world, Chief. Best in the world."

Backfire

Laurie Kolp

there is nothing aromatic
about the morning after
you hurled my head
into the choppy sea

it was like a cannon inside me
turned inside out &
the explosion set in motion
one more round

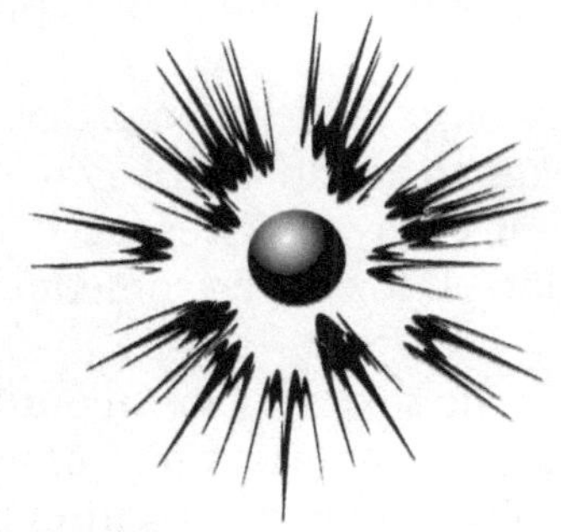

of drunken boldness
to break the silence
was like an unexpected flyover
setting into motion

cracks of joints and bone;
a mint scent not meant
to send me back to you
for a second smoky round

Black and White
(*and all of life's colors*)

Nikki Rohira

(Special thanks to Megha Ellathvalapil)

Life is full of black and white
as well as a mixture
of gray and hues.

Melting in the pot of sadness
and rising with the flame of happiness

It's okay to feel a black day,
it's okay to be sad, it's okay to cry,
it's okay to disrespect
yourself for loving someone.

Black is the sexiest color in our lives
and is an important part of us;
the black hollowness within us
actually completes us.

You don't need to realize who you are
to turn the tables;
sometimes you just need
to go with the flow.

If you only try to realize who you are,
how you can learn to be better?

Accept your defeats,
because they are actually
silent white victories,
paving the way for a colorful start.

Life is just a game of
colors and thoughts.

If you want to learn to be a better you,
forget the old you, and welcome your defeats
and challenges with open arms.

There is no such thing as undeserving.

You are served only what you are
ready to accept, and you are worthy of
whatever you wish.

Never regret anything, because
everything you might regret was
probably once the most
flamboyant shade of your life;

be it your dreams, your choices,
or loving someone near and dear.

Life has a complete variety of colors
embedded in black and white outlines;
embrace them all with love.

To all those who want revenge for their pasts,
those who hate their partners for ditching them,
those who regret their career choices,
and those who are upset and feeling unappreciated...

Remember that life is beautiful,
and while it sometimes seems like a
blend of only black and white

it is actually a rainbow
of all the beautiful
colors of creation.

Greymoor Hall

Dusty Grein

Dust lies thick in empty hallways;
as the light begins to fade
chill wind swirls down ancient chimneys,
cold and dry as brittle bone.

The old mansion lies uneasy,
knowing dues must still be paid.
Even though there is no movement
in its rooms, it's not alone.

For the restless souls who died here
have been trapped, and still remain,
and the house—once filled with laughter—
has grown evil and insane;
now no happiness is found here,
only anguish, fear, and pain.

In the attic is a nursery
used by little ones no more,
where abandoned in one corner
sits a broken china doll;

while the bowels of the building
hold a pit in earthen floor.
From this well without a bottom,
comes the curse of Greymoor Hall.

There was a time before the curse fell,
when the house was newly made—
standing strong against the weather,
its foundation solid stone—

there was light and there was laughter,
and here children gaily played.
Often music could be heard, as peaceful
moonlight sweetly shone,

every season was spent happy
in the sun, and snow, and rain
but the house, once filled with love,
has now completely gone insane,
for its memories of those years,
although skewed, are yet retained.

It remembers distant yesterdays,
bright waves upon a shore,
but a dark and evil undertow
has clouded its recall.

The despair of hope abandoned
is a throaty distant roar
from the well without a bottom,
in the heart of Greymoor Hall.

In those days, dear Anna Carver
was a sweet and buxom maid,
but her love for young Paul Greymoor
meant the seeds of death were sown,

for she gave to him her flower.
In the basement dirt they laid;
there the final drop of virgin blood,
was spilled with breathy moans,

and her sacrifice of innocence,
into the well did drain.
Soon the house was filled with screaming
and the sound drove it insane,
as the ductwork rang with echoes
and the walls with blood were stained.

Bittersweet, her loss of purity
had opened up a door;
in the depths of Hell, a demon
turned its head, answered the call

on its face an evil grin emerged,
as if it knew the score.
From the well without a bottom,
it climbed in to Greymoor Hall.

These young lovers were the first two
upon whom the demon preyed,
and their ravaged bodies, still alive,
into the pit were thrown

ere the monster threw its head back,
darkly laughed a cannonade,
and the solid walls around it
seemed to buckle and to groan.

Darkness gushed forth from the well,
like blood out of an open vein;
as the house filled up with evil,
all its dreams became insane
and the stench of death and decay
simply could not be contained.

Through the other living residents'
weak flesh the demon tore.
With the ending of their lives,
the final barrier did fall,

these environs were inhabited
by living souls no more
and the well without a bottom
held full sway at Greymoor Hall.

Near a century has passed now
since that unholy parade
and the grounds around the building
lie weed-choked and overgrown.

Faded wallpaper sags, peeling;
window coverings are frayed,
and once lustrous marble fixtures
now lie shattered and flyblown.

In the ballroom jet black spiders
and white maggots darkly reign,
while the basement, full of shadows,
echoes laughter quite insane
and this sound which can't be heard,
is one that science can't explain.

Faintly glowing in the moonlight
are green putrid fungus spores
which reflect upon the insects
who 'cross ancient remains crawl

near the blood red evil light source
which shines forth, a blighted sore
from the well without a bottom,
far below old Greymoor Hall.

It is said the ghosts of Anna
and Paul Greymoor, though insane

are still haunting rooms and hallways
now grown wicked to the core,
and the demon they set free that day
still lives within the walls;

Any humans who set foot inside,
will find out what's in store,
and the well without a bottom
will be fed in Greymoor Hall.

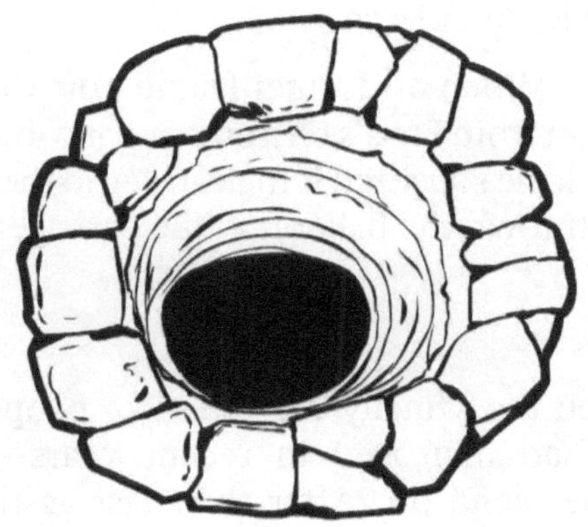

Kids, Cats and Quick Exits

Melodie Corrigall

For Larry, choosing between Trixie and his balloons was the most wrenching decision he had ever faced. Trixie was close to perfection, with her bouncy blond curls, soar in the sky smile, and understanding heart. He'd do anything for her . . . anything that is but give up his balloons.

He had collected his first balloon (long since buried) years earlier, the day he bought the house. A sizable basement room was now dedicated to them. They needed the entire room because Larry could not—and who but a heartless thug could—kill them. No matter how old and weak a balloon got, the thin pastel plastic stretched and bulging, he couldn't pierce it.

Others did. When his former friend Tom discovered an elderly balloon from Fred's retirement party hiding behind a chair at work, he squeezed it to death. And then, to Larry's horror, he'd thrown the balloon in the garbage as if it were nothing.

Not Larry.

Even when they finally did die—like people, their life expectancy had increased in recent years—Larry gave them a proper send off. After their last gasp, they were sorted by color or design so they could be with their own, and placed in a small metal box by his window.

Now he was faced with a choice: Trixie or his balloons. Struggle as he might, Larry couldn't come up with any way to save his balloons and meet Trixie's three points of con-tention: kids, cats and speedy exits. First, Trixie wanted kids, and he wasn't against it. If he had five hands he would sign up; as it was, when they went for a walk, his two hands were occupied: Trixie with one hand, his balloon with the other. Having lost his first love (a red helium balloon) he was terrified of losing another love—Trixie.

The cliché about the first love being the strongest was true. His was a shiny red balloon with a thin golden ribbon, and was so plump he could hardly get his arms around it. As soon as the balloon had been bestowed on him, Larry had lost interest in the birthday party: the other children swooping around playing airplane, the treat bags stuffed with plastic toys and gummy candies, the mothers clucking that it was time to leave. He'd raced outside, swinging his balloon, which in the breeze was as wild as he. It tugged to be free, to join the clouds.

He hurried ahead of his mother, who hesitated to shout thanks to Mrs. Bean and then called to him, "Larry, careful, hold on, hold on."

As he turned towards her, his hand opened and whoosh, his everything exploded into the air. "Mommy," he cried in horror watching, his heart rising. "Mommy, get it."

Larry had jumped and stretched his thin arms as far as he could, but the balloon was already flying high. He watched in agony as it shrank smaller and smaller.

"Mommy," he cried angrily, "Get my balloon!"

His mother put her arm around his bony shoulder. "It's gone, Larry."

"I want it back," he said, stamping his feet on the icy sidewalk.

"It's gone to play with the clouds," she said.

Larry stared into the sky stretching his head so far back it threatened to snap off. "Come back, come back. I want you, Balloon," he cried in his fierce thin voice, but it refused to come back. Instead, it got tinier and tinier, until it was the size of a marble, and then it disappeared.

Years had passed since that terrible event, but still, whenever Larry left the house with his chosen balloon, he held it tight and as he also loved Trixie, he held her tight too. Of course, she was too heavy to float away, but he could hardly show more concern for his balloon than for his lady-love.

In the early days, when he took Trixie's hand as they left the house, she swang his arm and cried, "We're like Parisian lovers walking along Rileyville streets hand in hand." Recently, however, she sometimes tried to break loose in order to window shop or dash across the street to talk with a friend.

But back to the problem of kids. Larry wasn't against the idea of having them but if he and Trixie had a kid he'd want to hold his or her hand and that would mean giving up Trixie's hand and if he had two kids or twins, well that would be impossible. They could never leave the house.

In a sense, he had his kids, there in the basement.

That was another problem: space. Trixie argued, "We wouldn't have to move. The baby could have the basement room." If that happened, where were his balloons supposed to go?

When Trixie wasn't talking kids, she was talking cats. Another no-no. If they had a cat, and it got into the basement, it might bang the balloons around, or worse, it might rip the very life from them with its sharp claws.

No way, no animals.

He had tried to address Trixie's third concern: slow exits. "You're so poky leaving the house," she complained. "I'm tired of pacing the pavement waiting for you, rain or shine."

His mother had sided with Trixie, suggesting he plan ahead. But how could he? He never knew what the day would be like. For example, his red shirt might look good with the yellow balloon in the dim light of the basement (he had tried to install better lights; they didn't help) but once he got outside, he could see that his outfit didn't do the yellow balloon credit; somehow the light was too bright, or too dull. Other times as soon as they got outside he noted the wind, and realized he had brought a balloon that was too large or shaped such that it would struggle in the breeze and the whole afternoon would be spent tugging and yanking and no one would enjoy that.

"Bloody twenty minutes yesterday, and fifteen today," Trixie said. "You manage to leave on time for work."

Of course he could. Workdays he only had to choose a balloon to match his orange overalls—standard uniform at Buckley's—and the balloon would be mostly indoors so he didn't have to worry about strong winds.

So those were the issues: kids, cats and quick exits.

He and Trixie had fought around and around this mulberry bush for four weeks, until yesterday, when Trixie threatened that if he didn't budge by morning, she was gone. Her suitcase (tissue paper between the layers of clothes to avoid creases) placed by the door, spoke of her determination.

The previous night had been the worst of Larry's life. He loved Trixie, with her perky nose and a laugh that would stop a van, but what would life be without his balloons?

In the small hours, unable to sleep, he had visited the balloons a number of times. (He watched them in the dim nightlight, not putting on the overhead light, which would disturb their rest.)

As he opened their door, they rustled and shifted about, restless in their sleep just like Trixie often was.

That's something he'd miss if she left, her moving quietly beside him, the warmth of her soft haired arm across his chest and the curve of her back as she cuddled against him. But it was too late for second thoughts; it was morning. Trixie had seen his note and she was moving around upstairs. The basement door creaked open.

"That's it, Larry," she shouted. "This is goodbye!"

He was stung. He couldn't bear to climb the stairs to see her off. He'd left a note to say he loved her but that, just like the movie stars, their differences were "irreconcilable."

Standing with his balloons around him like a multicolored skirt, Larry peered out the grimy basement window.

Trixie's feet jogged down the front stairs and headed up the walk. She was wearing her favourite "cheer me up" red pumps and his breath caught as he watched the tiny heels clip away. When she got to the sidewalk, she turned back.

Would she relent? No, she merely shrugged.

Behind him, in loving support, his balloons clustered—all ages, all shapes, all colors. Had it not been for their constancy, he couldn't have faced Trixie's departure.

He reached out his hand to caress his new silver CONGRATULATIONS balloon, so cool to the touch. Over his shoulder he glimpsed his elderly THANKS balloon, loyal and resplendent in gold and green.

Down the street Trixie tripped along, her shiny crimson shoes getting smaller and smaller just like that fateful red balloon had done, those many years ago.

Finally, all he could see were the heels, and then . . . nothing.

He'd always intended to make a contingency plan for his balloons in case of his death.

Now that Trixie was gone, he would move that to the top of his list.

My Dark Place

John Grey

It's dark and I'm nervous.
And the dogs barking makes it worse.
Then they stop and I tremble even more from the silence.
There's no light to back me up in this.
And the sun has gone off to reassure people
on the other side of the world.

I can't go to bed
because I know I won't sleep.
And no way I've leave the house.
I've no idea what's out there waiting for me.
A cat down in the alley lets out
a long screechy howl.
And there's someone patrolling the sidewalk
though I can't see his face.
No moon of course.
There never is in this part of town.

It's dark and I'm reduced
to my fears, my frailties.
I can't even convince myself
that I'm too much of a nobody
for the demons, the boogie men, to bother.

For I'm the only one in this house,
in this room, in this body.
When it comes to terrifying someone,
I'm the only alternative.

I start muttering to myself
as if whatever's out there
will mistake the sounds for company.
But whatever's in here knows better.
And it's a dark place
too dark for me to talk my way out of.

The Drink

Ron Wilson

Klaxons wailed, and the flashing red lights gave the massive room a feeling of impending disaster.

"Sven, what exactly are we looking at?" William asked.

"I could tell you what I *think* it might be, but you would not like what I have to say on the matter," Sven said, his thick Swedish accent seasoning his words.

Sven Gustafson and William Randolph stood behind the reinforced glass of the observation deck. It looked out over a million square feet of underground concrete super-structure. The two watched as whatever it was seeped out.

"It's dark," William said. Dark being the only word he could come up with.

"Ya. Very dark," Sven said. "But you say it as though you meant some kind of object, ya?"

"Okay . . ." William said, not sure if that's what he meant or not. "It looks like some kind of chain reaction to me."

"More like a dissolution reaction," Sven said. "But different, in that it appears to be on a quantum level."

The liquid obsidian that leaked from the acceleration tube, spread over the equipment, floor, walls, and ladders like black on smoldering paper. It spread out in a perfect sphere, engulfing whatever it touched; the leading edge like a digitized laser--sharp, but distorted with bright flashes of red particles.

"Remind me again why we work at the LHC," William said.

"The Hadron Collider's purpose is to boldly seek out what makes the universe tick," Sven said. "To discover the machinations that hold physical reality together. To explore the unanswered questions of quantum physics." As he spoke, he stared at the spreading darkness, his face expressionless. Resigned.

"Sven, I didn't want the LHC's goddamned mission statement. I wanted to know why the hell we're standing less than a hundred yards from where some of the smartest assholes in history are trying to make a black hole."

Sven said nothing.

"Sorry Sven," William said. "I don't think you're an asshole. Just those other guys."

"I do not believe we have succeeded in creating a singularity . . . but we have, I think, begun a most unfortunate event in our present space-time continuum."

"I . . . don't know what that means," William said. "Lowly electrician, remember?"

Sven sighed. "No, my friend. No black hole. I think, however, that we might have accidentally pulled out a very important stitch in the very fabric of creation."

"Uh . . . that doesn't sound good."

Sven huffed in ironic amusement. "Look closely at the center," he said, pointing through the glass towards the spreading blackness. In its wake, there was nothing. But it was an active nothing. A void so empty it seemed energetic.

William caught a glimpse of movement, and. . . *light*?

"Sven, what is that?"

"I have a theory, but I cannot be sure."

"So, let's have the theory."

"I believe it is an alternate reality."

A sharp burst of laughter escaped William. He didn't like the way it sounded. He cleared his throat, then said, "You think we're looking through some kind of doorway into another part of what . . . the multiverse?"

When Sven spoke, his voice had a distant, droning quality. "No, not a door; doors can be closed. I think we may have destroyed the entire wall."

The light grew brighter, more defined. It began as a sickly green hue. William thought it nothing like green, but he had no reference point to equate it with anything else. Obscene was close. Not right, but close. Abhorrent? Alien? Unlike any possible color in his world. "What color is that?" he asked.

"I'm not sure it can be classified as a color," Sven said. "Our eyes are specialized antennae that discern dissimilar electro-magnetic frequencies and transmute them into electro-chemical stimuli tha—"

"Got it Sven," William said. "Not a color."

They stared in silence, leaning forward until their foreheads almost touched glass.

William jumped back and let out a small chirp of a scream. "Okay. Just what the hell was that?"

Sven said nothing.

"Sven?"

Sven turned slowly and walked to his desk. He mechanically opened a drawer and pulled out a pistol.

"Sven," William said through clenched teeth. "Did your wife put marijuana in those brownies we ate this morning? Because I just saw some shit."

Calmly, Sven walked back to the window and stood next to his friend.

"Ya, William. I saw."

"How can we stop it?"

"Stop what, exactly?"

"The dissolution thingy?"

"The dissolution reaction?" Sven said. "Like I said, that is not a completely accura—"

"Yeah, yeah. Whatever," William said, exasperated. "Can we stop it?"

"We cannot. Theoretically it will continue on to the farthest reaches of our universe."

"What are we going to do?"

Sven looked on, silently stroking the pistol.

"Sven, we have to do something."

The not-green hue became more defined. More grotesque. As it did, William could feel rationality slipping away. What he saw was an abomination to his psyche. Vile, repulsive, and beautifully terrifying. He wasn't hardwired to accept it, to perceive it.

Another movement. This time William and the stoic Sven screamed together.

A beast flashed into existence, then out again. Quickly, but long enough for a few more tethers to break loose from the anchor of sanity that barely held the men.

Then more beasts. Creatures flying, swimming, running about on a firmament he could not comprehend. William wanted to run away, to escape. At the same time, he wanted to run towards the void, to offer himself to the inconceivable. To the inevitable.

To get it over with.

"Can they come across?" William said.

"There is no point," Sven said, his hand still contemplating the pistol.

"What do you mean?" William said. Then put up his hand. "In layman's terms please."

"We are unraveling. Disintegrating. Soon there will be nothing to come across to."

The charred fringes of chaos advanced in all directions.

The Klaxons stopped sounding, because they didn't exist any longer. There were no workers, no machines now.

Only extra-dimensional filled space before them.

"What do you think?" William asked. "Two minutes?"

"Ya. Given the current rate of discorporation, I think we have approximately two minutes before the leading edge of physical unreality reaches us."

"See? That's what I mean," William said. "How in the hell do you just come up with that off the top of your head?"

Sven shrugged. "Mm. It's a gift I guess."

"Do you want a drink?"

"William, I am a coward."

"Alcohol can help with that."

Sven handed William the pistol. "I cannot do this. I would ask you as a friend to help me," Sven said.

William's first instinct was to refuse, to tell him it would be okay; there would be a way out of their predicament.

But he knew better. "Yeah. I'll help you out. How many bullets?"

"The Glock 19 has a ten round capacity. I have loaded this with ninety-two grain pre-fragmented sel—"

William stopped him by putting a hand on his shoulder. With the other he gently took the pistol. "I got it man. Ten rounds."

Sven said. "You will be able to ah . . . help me, and then help yourself, ya?"

The two men stood in silence and watched approaching doom. "I am sorry I cannot help you my friend," Sven said.

William sighed. "That's okay buddy. You theoretical types aren't known for your practical skills." He pulled a flask from his coat pocket. "How about that drink?"

"Ya. Thank you."

Sweet Memories

Laurie Kolp

I recall floating out
of a donut floatie
when my father
forced me to swim

my false sense of security
forgotten
with each arm spin
and fast kick

then there was the
360 degree skid I did
on a slick road
in a rush
back to work

I almost missed my late twenties
only to discover my love for
warm glazed pregnancy days
a haze from guilty pleasures

chocolate éclair
if I dared to splurge
cinnamon twist and
blueberry cake

I'd make my husband
wake at 5 a.m.
just to get the freshest batch

I don't want to forget
teacher work days
where we'd be greeted with
donuts and coffee
or midnight surprises
after nights on the town

donuts now winding
down to my hips,
an added tire
worthy of the joy
it took to get there

not to mention thin and crisp
outside-the-box apple fritters
like Mother craved
each day before she died

not one, but two
because who cared
about healthy living
anymore

The Wind River Story

Steve Carr

As the car slowed, the wind against Dan's face began to feel less like a hurricane. Although he was aware of the grit being blown in through the back window, it wasn't the dirt in his face that was bothering him, it was the gun being aimed at him that was irritating.

Dan didn't like guns, especially guns that were pointed at him, even if they were small. This one was only a pistol, but being unfamiliar with guns—other than the damage they could do—he had no idea what kind of pistol it was. It didn't really matter; as he stared at the barrel, he was certain the last thoughts of most people just before they were shot, were not about the type of gun that was pointed at them.

This was Dan's first actual encounter with a gun, and other than sitting still and letting his face be sandblasted by the incoming grit, he wasn't certain how to react. He tried his best not to react at all, but the beads of perspiration running down his tanned forehead were telling another story.

He could have told the young woman, Erica, not to shoot him, that he didn't want to die, but as those words played out in his head, they seemed like an overstatement of the obvious, so he said nothing.

Erica was in the front passenger seat and was turned toward Dan in the back seat, the pistol firmly in her grasp. She seemed to know a lot about pistols—at least about the pistol she was aiming at him—because she had already told him in no uncertain terms how easy it would be for her to put a bullet between his baby blue eyes.

The car was slowing, as were the cars in front and behind. They had come about five miles south of Thermopolis, into the Wind River Canyon. The past five miles had been, without a doubt, the most hair raising five miles of Dan's entire life. His anxiety threatened to send him into a grand mal-like seizure, so to calm himself he bit into his tongue behind sealed lips.

He could still taste the blackberry pie he had eaten just before sticking out his thumb and heading south along the Wind River. He'd left South Dakota, crossed Wyoming into the Grand Tetons, traveled through Big Horn National Park, then made his way southward, without any damage to his body or soul, other than an encounter with a bee the day before with a gun of its own, which it had used on Dan's forearm. It was the diminishing pain of the bee sting and the taste of blackberry pie that he tried to concentrate on; thinking about Erica and her pistol only increased the amount of sweat his body was producing.

A blackberry seed, lodged between his molars, had drawn the attention of his tongue. Try as he might, keeping his tongue from causing unwanted movement of his mouth was getting more difficult by the moment. He turned his attention to the memory of the delicious blackberry pie he had escaped with, from that diner in Thermopolis.

Other than a name on his wrinkled map, Dan knew nothing about Thermopolis, except what the driver of the Chevy pick-up who dropped him there had told him. "It has hot springs. It's what draws the tourists."

The driver had said little else, preferring to spend his time singing along to the Golden Oldies blaring on the radio. When he pulled over at the northern end of Thermopolis, he'd said "This is it." He didn't just mean it was the beginning of

Thermopolis, but also that it was the end of the ride. Dan had gotten out of the car, retrieved his backpack from the truck bed, and thanked the driver, before adjusting the shoulder straps and continuing on foot in the same direction.

It was one of those rules of hitchhiking. You didn't ask why a driver picked you up, or why they decided to dump you alongside the road, still heading the same direction you wanted to go. It was their vehicle and their rules; you just played along, unless, of course, the situation called for a quick escape from a crazy driver. This one had been nice enough, although a bit too intense, mostly non-verbal, and apparently a bit hard of hearing.

Entering Thermopolis on foot had its advantages. Dan had hoped to get a glimpse of the springs, but the closest he came was a billboard pointing in their direction. It was mid-day and a haze hung over all of Thermopolis, subduing all color, and making the high humidity feel more smothering than it might on a clear day.

By the time he reached the diner near the mouth of the canyon, Dan was hungry, thirsty and dirty. The soothing and cleansing results of the bath he had taken in the cold stream in the Big Horns the day before, had worn off and a diner—with a good menu and a bathroom with a working sink—was exactly what he needed.

Entering the diner, the first thing he noticed was that the few customers seated at the tables and the two waitresses waiting on them were elderly, or near it. The little bell above the door tinkled rather loudly, and they all turned and looked at Dan as he entered. He found an empty table at the window looking out onto the street, undid his backpack, and placed it on the floor beside his chair. He sat down and opened the menu, scanning the sandwiches section.

One of the waitresses, her white hair swirling about her head like soft vanilla ice cream and dressed in a pale pink uniform, came up to his table. She stood looking at him for a moment before saying anything.

"You a movie star?" she asked.

"No," Dan answered, "why do you ask that?"

"I thought maybe they were making a movie nearby. They do that sometimes, make movies here, those Hollywood people, and you look like a movie star."

"Thank you," he said, blushing.

"It wasn't a compliment," the waitress said brusquely. She took her order pad out of a pocket in her apron and pulled a small pencil from her behind her ear. "What'll you have?"

Dan ordered a roast beef sandwich with potato salad, a large Coke and a piece of blackberry pie. As the waitress walked away, he looked for the restroom. Seeing the men's sign on a door near the back of the diner, he shoved his backpack under the table and headed for it.

It was glaringly white; everything in it was painted a brilliant white and smelled as sterile as it looked. Dan wanted to lock the door, but it had no lock so he took his chances. He stood at the small sink and removed his shirt, placing it on a small radiator before pumping some hand soap onto a paper towel and running it under the water. He raised his left arm and wiped his underarm; he was about to do the same with his right one, when the door opened and an elderly man came in, wearing a red flannel shirt, jeans, cowboy boots, and a white Stetson. The old man stopped briefly when he saw Dan, then went to the urinal and unzipped his pants. Dan continued soaping his right underarm.

"Don't let them catch you doing that in here," the man said as he peed into the urinal.

Surprised that he was being spoken to, Dan hesitated for a moment before replying. "Is there a law against cleaning up in a restroom?"

"Not a law," the old man said. " Just frowned on. People around here are peculiar about those kinds of things. As the saying goes, forewarned is forearmed."

"Thanks for letting me know," Dan said, wiping the soap from his underarm and tossing the wet paper towel in the small trash basket. As Dan put his shirt on, the old man stood at the urinal looking at him, and was still watching him as he walked out of the restroom.

The food, including the piece of pie and the coke, was on his table when Dan returned. He sat down, bit into the sandwich, and washed it down with some Coke. He became lost in thought and didn't realize the old man from the restroom was now standing by the table, quietly watching him. The man sneezed and Dan looked up from his plate of food, saying automatically "Bless you."

"I got a place you can clean up at," the old man said.

"Oh, thanks but I am on a schedule and need to get back on the road as soon as I'm done eating."

"My place ain't far from here," the old man said. "Not much there, other than my trailer and a carrot patch, but I got an outdoor shower and no one ever comes around." The man looked around, then bent down closer to Dan's ear, "You can even sleep over if you have a mind to."

Not certain about the meaning, or implication, of the old man's invitation, Dan bit into his sandwich again and swallowed before replying. Dan didn't consider himself homophobic, and at times felt almost ambiguous about his own sexual identity, but there, in that diner—in Thermopolis of all places—the possibility he was being propositioned by another man caused him to lose the ability to respond with anything along the line of sanity. He said, jokingly, "If I did, I'd have to kill you."

From the reaction on the old man's face it was apparent he didn't take it as a joke, and stepping back very quickly from Dan's table, he collided with the waitress and they both fell against a standing coat rack; all three—man, waitress, coat rack—falling to the floor. The stunned reactions of the other diners gave Dan enough time to pull money from his shirt pocket and put it on the table, grab his backpack in one hand, the piece of pie off the plate in the other, and depart the diner unnoticed.

Dan quickly walked toward the mouth of the Wind River Canyon, and what looked like a scenic overlook. This spot allowed tourists to peer down at the Wind River, rushing far below, or down the canyon at the rocky cliffs. Railroad tracks ran along one side, and US 20 carried traffic going into and out of the canyon on the other. Along the way, Dan stuffed the entire piece of pie in his mouth, and while enjoying the sweet taste of blackberries—and enduring the tiny seeds getting caught in between his perfect teeth—he put his backpack on, leaving the straps unbuckled.

He turned and stuck out his thumb at a safe spot near the overlook, hoping to get out of Thermopolis with greater speed then he had gone through it. It wasn't that anything as bad as the bee sting had happened, really. It was just the feeling he had, that something bad would happen.

On the other side of the river, a freight train was moving slowly down the tracks. Back in Spearfish, South Dakota, a friend had suggested to Dan that taking trains and riding boxcars all the way to San Francisco might be more fun, and safer, than thumbing across country; now watching the train, Dan wished he had done as his friend had suggested.

A car pulled up beside him, and a teenage girl with bright, curly, red hair stuck her head out. "We're going south just like you, if you want a ride, but you got to be okay with open windows, cause they don't roll up on this side."

Dan leaned down and peered into the car. With the teen girl was a woman of about forty, with long straight black hair parted down the middle, wearing large hoop earrings. The left side of her face was bruised purple and black, and her lower lip was slightly swollen.

"That's my mom," the girl said, nodding in the woman's direction. "She don't always look like that. She had an accident." The girl paused briefly. "You want a ride or not?"

Dan looked back over his shoulder at the train entering the canyon, then said, "Sure." He opened the back door, threw in his backpack and climbed in, settling back as the woman pulled onto the road, merging with the steady stream of southbound traffic.

"I'm Dan," he said, as the girl turned toward him in her seat.

"I'm Erica, and she's Lucy," the girl said, giving Dan the once-over from his dusty hiking boots to the top of his sandy brown hair. "You running from something?"

The question seemed an odd one but slightly funny. "No, why would you ask that?"

"Guys who hitchhike along this way always seem to be running from something. Mama says it's the nature of this canyon, that it draws men into it who are on the run from something." Erica placed her hand on her mother's shoulder. "Isn't that what you always say Mama?"

Lucy didn't answer, but kept her eyes on the road ahead, her cheek muscles visibly tightening and loosening beneath the purple bruise. She was gripping the steering wheel so tightly, the blue veins on the back of her hands stood out like lines on a map.

"Mama says it sucks men in one end, and spits them out at the other."

"I'm just kind of sightseeing on my way to California," Dan said. He wasn't certain, but suspected that what he was smelling on Erica's breath was alcohol of some sort, but in the rush of air and dust coming in through the open window, he doubted his sense of smell.

"What's that blue stuff on your upper lip?" Erica asked him, pointing with a bright pink polished nail.

Dan giggled, sounding more effeminate than he intended, then rubbed the back of his hand beneath his nose. "I had some blackberry pie, and didn't know I got it on me."

"Blackberry pie!" Erica and Lucy said in unison, and Erica suddenly reached into her waistband and pulled out the pistol, aiming it at Dan's face. "He give you that pie?" She snarled, baring her teeth.

"He, who?"

"You know who. Him. He give you that pie?"

"I got it at a diner in Thermopolis," Dan said.

"Liar," Lucy screamed without turning around or taking her eyes off the road.

"Liar," Erica repeated.

"No, really. I got it at a diner. Why would someone give me blackberry pie way out here?"

Erica leaned over and whispered into Lucy's ear, without taking the pistol from Dan's face.

Ahead the cars slowed, and Lucy slowed their car also. Dan glanced out the window, looking down at the dark green water flowing rapidly through the canyon, when something caught his eye. A large white bird, a seagull in flight headed southward. The sight of the seagull so surprised him, that momentarily he forgot there was a pistol aimed at his head. Seagulls didn't belong this far inland. The only thing he really knew about seagulls was that they were coastal birds. He wanted to share his surprise at seeing it with someone, anyone, like a secret that had to be told, but when he turned back to face Erica, she still had the pistol pointed at him and was scowling.

"My step daddy was coming this way this morning. He drives an old Chevy pick-up. He gave you that blackberry pie, didn't he? It was some sort of pay off to not tell us you had seen him, wasn't it?"

There were so many holes in the logic of the question, that Dan didn't know where to begin. His tongue found the seed between his molars, and working feverishly finally dislodged it. Dan turned his head and spat the seed out the window. Across the river, the freight train had partially come off the tracks, and several freight cars were on their sides on the rocky bank. The engine was partially submerged in the rushing water.

"Damn, Mama! Look at that," Erica said, seeing the train but keeping the pistol aimed at Dan.

Lucy had slowed the car to the snail's pace of all the other cars, onlookers to the unbelievable sight of a train partly on its side along the Wind River. "Nothing good ever comes from going into this canyon," she said.

~

About forty minutes later, with Erica still pointing her pistol at Dan's head, they came out of the south end of the canyon into an open vista—the Boysen Reservoir and a bright blue sky.

Dan had grown accustomed to the pistol. He didn't like it any more than before, but had become used to the idea that Erica got some perverse pleasure out of pointing it at him. As the hot breeze flowed in through the open windows, Dan looked out over the reservoir, and there they were, more seagulls, circling above the reservoir.

The land all around seemed bereft of trees, or anything green for that matter; also absent was law enforcement.

The cars, including the one he was in, exited the canyon and quickly increased to race car speeds, all the way to—and through—the small town of Shoshone. This was where Lucy stopped the car.

Lucy turned her bruised face toward Dan. "Get out."

"Gladly," Dan said picking up his backpack from the floorboard.

"No, leave that," Lucy said. "It's payment for that stolen blackberry pie you ate with that bastard, my husband."

"Everything I own is in this backpack," Dan protested.

"You heard Mama," Erica said, waving the pistol in his face. "Leave the backpack, or I swear to God I will shoot you, right here and now."

Dan opened the car door and stepped out onto a broken sidewalk, along what looked to be an abandoned brick building. The sun was glaring, and Dan squinted at Erica as she closed the car door.

He stood watching as Lucy did a U-turn and sped off northward, back toward the canyon and Thermopolis. He felt like crying, but the immaturity of doing that when it served no purpose kept him from it, so he kicked at the dirt on the sidewalk, and sat down.

The brick wall behind him had been nicely painted with Native American graffiti—young Indian boys around a campfire.

Dan felt lucky he still had the money in his wallet, but looking down the street of mostly abandoned buildings, he didn't see anywhere he could buy even basic supplies: toothpaste, toothbrush, deodorant, shampoo.

When the same man in the Chevy pick-up who had given him a ride earlier pulled to a stop in the middle of the street, Dan had the disturbing thought he had gone insane. It passed quickly, and he sprang to his feet.

"Hey, we meet again," the man said matter-of-factly.

"Your wife is looking for you!" Dan said angrily. "She thought I ate some of the pie you stole, and she took my backpack, and left me stranded here."

"She knows about the pie, huh?" The man pushed the ball cap back on his head and scratched his balding scalp. "She didn't say anything about me slapping her around a bit did she?"

"No. She was only mad about the pie."

"I sure hope by the time I get home, she's calmed down. Her and that daughter of hers are crazy, but sometimes living with them has its thrills." The man gave Dan a quick wave, turned up his radio, and as a Golden Oldie blared, he pulled away and headed back north to the canyon.

Dan looked up at the sky, just as a seagull flew over, casting its shadow on the street. With a heavy sigh, he stuck out his thumb, waiting for his next ride. He only wanted to get far away from the Wind River Canyon, as fast as possible.

The Day of the Meteorite

John Grey

It's a crime scene
to end all crime scenes.
David slays Goliath,
except the boy king is a space rock,
and the giant is where we live.

One great explosion
and the world is suddenly uprooted
from its geography.
Its dust forms clouds.
Its innards gasp for air.
Fire goes right for the throat
of the inflammable.
Flames drop from the sky like paratroopers,
climb buildings in a single orange bound.

All is in turmoil.
Mountains implode.
Cities incinerate.
Plagues of insects
swarm each viable crumb of life.
Fish rise from boiling oceans.
Reptiles forge ahead with their plans.

Letters From Jenni

P.A. O'Neil

To my Dear Family,

Though this letter will bring little solace, know that I am all right. My trial and my pain, though excruciating, was brief and I am at peace. You don't understand, and possibly never will, why it happened and truthfully, I don't quite know myself. You raised me to be loving and strong, to see only the best in people. We went to church faithfully, had a supportive family, and considered our neighbors to be more than just friends. Why then was our family chosen for this heartache?

When you think back on that fateful morning, don't dwell on what you could've done different to prevent the tragedy. Yes, you might've made me stay home, or insisted I take another route, but those decisions were only links in the chain of events that was to occur. It wasn't your fault. If there is anyone to blame, blame me for being who I am, or who I was, daring, determined, competitive, and strong-willed.

It is a shame you weren't able to see me drive my first car or graduate from high school. Daddy, you will never walk me down the aisle, or you, Mama, have a grandchild to hold.

Allow yourselves to grieve, my dear mother, my loving father, but please do not hold on to any guilt. That emotion should not be yours to bear, though for years to come, it will hover like the shadow of a cloud over our home.

Have faith the truth will, one day, come to light and justice will be served, even though no man's justice will ever be able to return me to your arms. Until that day, and the day of your own passing, my dear ones, know one day, we'll be joined again as a family.

~

To my wonderful Friends,

Because of my tragedy, your childhood came to an abrupt and premature end. Your exposure to the ugly truth about the world outside our close-knit community came too soon because of my actions, my decisions.

Gone are the summers where everyone banded together as soon as the last sip of sugar sweetened milk was drunk from our cereal bowls. It was not uncommon to rotate from house to house at lunchtime. Riding bikes, shooting baskets, playing tag, and jumping rope were daily events where all participants weren't expected home until called to dinner, filthy from the day's activities.

But those days of bliss ended that fateful day when these treasured childhood experiences were brutally torn from our lives. Don't blame yourselves because none of you wanted to ride bikes that day. There is no way of knowing if what happened could've been prevented, or even compounded, if you had been there. After all, it was just another bike ride through the park.

It was a different age than the one you live in now, and I'm sorry for my contribution to that change. Your parents held you tighter than before, as you now hold your own children fast to your side. They will never know the era of innocence which you were rudely ripped from. You, my friends, must believe that there is a destination of peace, where we'll once more feel safe enough to ride our bikes alone in the park and stay out until the street lights come on.

~

To the Monster who murdered me,

You are referred to as a monster, as no decent man would've done what you did to me.

You planned my death well in advance, I was not just a random victim. Biking around the park was a common activity for children my age. Who knows, maybe you saw me while riding with your own children? Maybe that is why there was no fear when I stopped to say, "Good morning," or inquire, "Do you have a flat tire?" It doesn't matter now, because whatever it was, you took advantage of my naivety to pull me off my bicycle and drag me into the bushes.

Was there delight, when you held your hand over my mouth so I couldn't scream? Did my kicking amuse you? Were you excited when my fingernails scratched your face? Did my tears burn when they fell from my cheeks onto your hand? You held me down and took from me that which was not even mine to give yet, something I was far too innocent to understand was of such worth. But it didn't end there, did it?

After defiling my body, coward that you are, you slit my throat so I could never share this experience with the police. Did you stay and watch as the blood escaped my body, or in your cowardice, had you already turned tail and run? You might have left me behind to die, but you know the memory of what you did will stay with you until your eyes forever close, and God willing long after, as you burn in Hell.

The death sentence you bestowed on me, condemned you to an eternity of guilt. How long did it take for you to wash my blood off your hands? Did you hide your stained clothing from your wife? Did you continue to ride your bicycle in the park with your children, hurrying past that fateful spot, where you so cruelly denied my family the possibility of ever feeling whole again? My death by your hand was like a pebble thrown into a pond, the ripples reaching farther than your mind will ever conceive.

One day, you will be found. One day, you will be tried. One day, you will be convicted, but until the day you are found guilty of my rape and murder, I know that your conscience has already found you guilty, and your sentence is that I will haunt your soul, forever.

~

To my Gentle Reader,

Hold fast, have faith, and believe in justice, but at the same time be ever vigilant in the ways of monsters who look like men. These monsters live in houses and apartments just like yours; they have children who go to the same schools as yours; they probably shop at the same stores; and they may even pretend to worship where you do.

Does this mean you should trust no one? Of course not. What it does mean is that you need to be more watchful, get to know your neighbors and their children. Be more aware of your surroundings and consider how vulnerable you, and your loved ones, are in any situation. Times have changed. The carefree days of playing free, without supervision, is now just something depicted in the movies.

Above all, you must have faith. Faith in the criminal justice system, faith in your fellow man, and faith that whatever happens here on this Earth, will be set right again in Heaven.

Sincerely yours,
Jenni

Tequila Shots

Laurie Kolp

zingy air
that exquisite risqué ring
mixes innocence with lime

all movement of the lips
puckers me silent

if my mouth
could see
it would see you and me
peppered zesty

you would
satisfy my need
to watch your clothes fall off
like one unbroken strand of citrus peel

The Legacy of Lady Seltzer

Kent Swarts

If anyone had asked Nicu how he wound up laying on his face, in the wet sand of a streambed, he would have said, "I don't know," and he didn't. He awkwardly got to his feet and wiped blood from his nose and mouth while he looked around. He was in a desolate high valley with mountains in the background. His burned cycle lay five yards away, in several pieces.

He brushed damp sand off his shirt, and took a few hesitant steps toward the cycle when he noticed the bush next to him. It had been burned, and not just the leaves. The flowers and stems had also been charred, almost to the ground. "Damn, a mag-pulsar did that."

The walk back to Alamosa took him two days.

~

A few stores, and even fewer run-down shacks, dotted the remaining streets of the town. Families lived and ran strange businesses in tents, scattered across the nearby hillsides.

Nicu stopped at a run-down saloon and ordered whiskey to calm his nerves. *How many times had he been here to soothe his anger?*

After downing three shots, he left and walked to B's house—a small, dilapidated, wood-frame bungalow she had decorated with figurines cut from old planks. There was no glass in the window frames, but she had hung beach towels over them, providing color against the bare, sun-parched wood.

He went in without knocking, and sat at the small table that served for eating, sewing, woodworking, and hacking websites. B herself lay on her bed in the corner of the room with her feet propped up on a chair. She was not asleep, but almost out, cold, and sick. An empty Mason jar lay on the floor just out of her grasp.

"You need to do some shit, B."

"I did."

"No, some real shit. The kind that brings in food money."

"No one needs my skills."

He laughed and paused, staring at the splintered tabletop. "You know, we never were a thing."

"We could have been if it hadn't been for . . ." She turned her head away from Nicu. "Well, it no longer matters."

"Computer skill is what I want."

She slowly got to her feet with his help and together they walked outside, where she puked. "You gotta buy electricity."

"I'll get you a solar generator."

She chuckled. "You always promise me things you never deliver."

"I would have, but." He knew excuses were not something she cared about. "I'll be back tonight." He turned to leave, and she kissed his cheek. He walked away waving.

~

He returned at nine o'clock dragging a beat up solar generator with several broken or missing solar panels. "Has no charge, so we wait till morning."

"Where am I supposed to hide the damn thing? It'll be gone by morning."

"Under your goddamn bed, B. How would I know? I got shot at stealing the piece of junk. You could at least thank me."

"Thanks," she said far too dryly to suit him.

He walked away waving her off.

They both knew he'd be back; he always came back. His attachment to her was like a moth drawn to a flame, a fly drawn to a web, a deer in headlights. They had never slept together, but it was not for his lack of trying. She had a hold over him he did not understand, and it seemed she only toyed with him. She said she wanted room, and he guessed he wanted her to have her room, too. "Generators don't bind people." He kicked the dirt.

~

Morning came and went.

She walked to the bar looking for him, but the barkeep, Old Guss, said he hadn't been in. She drank a couple shots of tequila and left. She stopped at Smitty's Sporting Goods, but Dodge hadn't seen him either. At one time, Smitty's had been the largest sporting goods store in Southern Colorado; now it was poorly stocked. Dodge mostly sold odd guns—which he bought from people who needed cash for food—and used camping gear he picked up around the area. That, and gasoline. No one knew where he got it, but most days he put out a sign that read, "Fuel Cheap." It was anything but cheap.

A man neither Dodge nor she knew, stood in the corner looking at an old stuffed bobcat. He said, "Lean guy? Long brown hair, in a ponytail?"

"Yeah," said Dodge.

"He walked out of town this morning heading west. Said he hated this place."

"You and he talked?" she said.

"Naw. He did. I was on my way in with my wife and child."

"Newcomers?"

"Yes. So, what do you want for the bobcat?"

~

Nicu sat on the edge of a bluff, watching the road below. He hoped someone with a vehicle would come along. He needed a ride anywhere except back to Alamosa, but he hadn't seen a soul on that road. He thought about B and their strange relationship, but came no conclusions.

He climbed back down, walked to B's place, and sat on the front step. She arrived carrying a gunny-sack containing a few groceries.

"I suppose I have to fix you dinner."

"You don't have to, but it would be a friendly gesture. How's the gen?"

"Good. Boiled cabbage and hotcakes?"

"Sure."

"What do you want?"

"To know where I can buy a mag-pulsar."

"That's not what I meant. You have money for one?"

"No. Looking."

"Window shopping. Stupid."

"I was shot at with one."

"They had to be a pretty bad shot if you are still alive."

"Blew my cycle to shit."

"Come on in. I'll start dinner. You set the table." She held the screen door open for him, and then closed and latched the door. "You going to steal one?"

"Might. I'm going to get even."

"With whom?"

"The asshole that shot me."

"Who?"

"No idea, but people don't go around shooting others for no reason."

"Then it wasn't people."

He set two forks and two knives on the table. "The Seteks don't give a flip about us."

"They do if you pissed them off."

"I don't think I did, except . . . maybe last year."

Almost a year ago in Walsenburg, he had gotten into a fight with a Setek—which is what people called the hybrid children of those who mated with the aliens when they had 'visited' Earth. The aliens had looked much like Seth, the Egyptian god of disorder, and the Seteks had characteristics of both aliens and humans. Seteks were taller, thinner, and had longer extremities than true humans. Their eyes often bulged, but were different from the aliens, whose eyes were similar to frogs. A few Seteks had a narrow beak-like face and slightly webbed feet. Once the aliens had raped Earth—and many of its humans—they left. Nicu's bar fight with the Setek, had sent the hybrid to the hospital.

Nicu and B searched the Internet for three hours, and found four mag-pulsars for sale. None were affordable. One was owned by a Setek living in Salida, not too far away. Nicu decided on that one. He needed transportation to get to Salida, and he needed a loan.

The only person in town who had both the money and a vehicle, was Lady Isabella Seltzer. She lived in a rundown mansion on fifteen hundred acres northwest of town, where she raised cattle and sheep.

She gave food, clothing, and blankets to those less fortunate, and demanded little in return, although she did require some folks to protect her interests in exchange. Nicu was one of these, and she occasionally asked him to do additional things.

Proud, independent and business-like, Isabella had vibrant blue eyes, short-cropped brown hair, and long bony fingers. She walked tall, and talked taller. Her speech could charm a snake, or publically butcher a person. She had fed and clothed Nicu after his parents died.

He was not a loner, but he had no close friends, at the ranch or in town. He'd met B at the ranch, but she was only there a short time, before she left during a February blizzard. B was about as close as friends came.

Nicu decided to approach Lady Seltzer.

~

The next morning she listened to him, but disagreed with his reasons for wanting the pulse-gun. She would not support a vindictive use of the powerful weapon, but she said she would support its use to keep the peace. He was unable to grapple with the difference.

She suggested he change his point of view. "Don't seek revenge, seek ways you can help others survive the atrocities we see day in and day out."

"You want me to protect the town?"

"No, just those who use the roads around Alamosa. How many people are robbed at gunpoint or threatened by gangs, for no other reason than they can get away with it?" She took a sip of tea and said, "I'm not advocating you become a vigilante, only that you rid the roads around here of thieves."

Nicu did not agree with her interpretation of vigilante, but if she would meet his needs, he could nod the right way.

"I don't think you understand what I'm saying," she said. "For example, wolves attack my young cattle. I can kill wolves, but more show up. I could build wolf-proof fences, but at what cost? Therefore, to protect the greatest number, I separate two calves from the herd and the wolves are satisfied. They kill one and later the other, and then move on. We both win. That is what I am advocating."

"I believe I understand. I should become their prey."

"But, do it smartly."

~

The ranch foreman and three hands drove Nicu to Salida. The foreman paid cash for the mag-pulsar gun. When they returned to the ranch, Lady Seltzer handed Nicu the weapon and asked if he had a plan. He told her he planned to patrol two roads: Route 17 to the sand dunes, and the highway to Walsenburg. She told him he should camp with the travelers.

The problem he faced was that the weapon was far too powerful and unfocused to be used around those he was supposed to protect. He needed a sidekick with a standard weapon. Nicu went back to B's because she was good with ideas. He told her his problem.

She brought two shot glasses and a bottle of tequila to the table, and poured two shots. "No lime, no salt."

They downed the drinks and she poured two more. "A family moved to town yesterday. The guy bought that old stuffed bobcat from Dodge, set it in the street, and his daughter blasted it to pieces with a pump-action, sawed-off shotgun. She is the sidekick you want."

"She shoots stuffed animals?"

"She can shoot. Her dad said she killed game for them on their way here."

~

Jaelle Swift leaned against a fence-rail, sighting the mag-pulsar. The weapon weighed nearly twenty pounds; not many people could hold and aim it without support. She fired. A whirring sound emanated from the forks, and an instant later a nearby 55-gallon drum disintegrated. "Awesome," she said.

Nicu smiled. He guessed that the girl, tall and fair skinned, was about sixteen or seventeen. Her hair, while unruly and frazzled, was a golden blonde and fell below her broad shoulders. She had bony cheeks, bony knees and wore tennis shoes with holes in the toes and heels. She neither smiled nor scowled, and she squinted. "So?"

"You want the job?"

"I've never actually killed a person, but I guess there is a first. Sure. My dad said you told him you'd pay?"

"Not a lot, but it will put food on the table."

~

The two set off up Route 17 in Lady Seltzer's Jeep, to where an old dirt road joined from the west. This had been the location of Moska, but the town no longer existed; people had torn its few buildings apart to build fires. The only marks now in the intersection were those of horses and carts. East of the junction in the sandy dirt, a few scattered remains of campfires and trash littered the ground.

Nicu and Jaelle set up a camp protected from the road, built a small fire, and threw together a lean-to behind a sand dune. They saw nothing that night, but the next morning he paid her.

They tore down camp and stowed their gear in the lean-to, drove across the desert, and spent the rest of the day exploring the dunes.

Sand Dunes National Park and Preserve had once been a tourist attraction. After the aliens, that changed.

The aliens had left the world in shambles, destitute and hungry. During the five years they were here, they scoured Earth taking anything they saw fit: goods, mineral resources, and foodstuffs, including poultry, beef, and pork. They were thorough.

Their giant spaceships had ringed the blue planet by the hundreds, and thousands of small ships made runs to Earth and back, transporting everything. What they didn't take they, demolished or damaged badly. Copper was especially important to them, and they had torn homes and commercial buildings apart to strip wire from them. They dismantled air conditioning units for the condensing copper coils. They stripped electrical plants, generating stations and smelters of the metal as well. During the horrible five years of looting, they mated forcefully—and occasionally agreeably—with humans, and they took everyone's dignity when they left.

The world starved and did without, people revolted, and governments toppled because they no longer had control. Around the world, national parks became relics of the past.

That night, Nicu and Jaelle set up camp a hundred yards further south, in the open. They started a fire, filled two shirts with brush, and put blankets around the shoulders.

Shortly before midnight, three people on horseback rode toward the camp. Two stopped at the junction while the third rode into the camp.

He looked around and hollered, "They don't got much!" He climbed off his horse, withdrew a rifle from its scabbard, and pointed it at the dummies. "Get your hands over your heads."

The other two rode up to him.

"Doesn't look right, Jed," said a feminine voice.

"No, it don't. Phil, check the tent."

Nicu aimed the mag-pulsar at Jed.

As Jed re-mounted, Nicu fired. The two men and their horses toppled. Before they hit the ground, Jaelle fired at the woman, wounding the horse. It stumbled, throwing the woman.

Jaelle ran toward her, reloading the shotgun. "Don't move, lady."

"I'm Bridgette," the woman said as she got to her knees and put both hands on her head.

Nicu approached her. "Are there more?"

"No." She looked at the burned men and horses. "The others are back in camp."

"Get up." He tied her hands behind her back and shoved her back down.

"Jaelle, fetch the pulse-gun and keep watch."

Nicu tore down the camp and recovered their gear, while Jaelle stood guard.

The three drove to Lady Seltzer's ranch, stopping near the entrance and waiting for the sun to rise before going in. Once daylight crept across the land, the three walked to the ranch house.

Lady Seltzer met them on the porch.

Jaelle said, "This is Bridgette. Two others are dead, and more are still back there."

"Hello, Bridgette. It has been a while."

"Hello, Aunt Issa."

"Take her to the small silo."

"You don't get it! They'll come for me."

"Who? Your brother, your cousin?"

"All of them."

Nicu stood with his mouth agape, staring at Lady Seltzer, then turned and led the woman away. There were things about Isabella Seltzer that still surprised him. He never knew she had a niece, nephew, or any other family—living or dead. He'd never asked, but during the time he lived at the ranch, and worked in her home, he never saw any pictures of family—not even of her husband, if she even had one.

When he returned, Jaelle was eating an ice-cream bar on the back porch. Seltzer paced and spoke intermittently to the foreman. "How many are there?" she asked Nicu.

"We don't know. Bridgette said more was all."

Jaelle finished the bar and said, "You want me to question your niece? I can."

"No. I'll talk with her later. She needs to fret a while." The lady paid Nicu, and asked for the blaster before they left.

~

Nicu gave Jaelle several gold coins, and thanked her for her help.

"Are we done, then?"

"You did good, Jaelle, but I have something else to do. Alone."

The two separated in town. Nicu rented a horse and rode off toward Walsenburg. When he reached Mt. Mestas he stopped and set up camp. He decided this was as good a place as any, if whoever had shot at him was still along the road.

He built a large fire and cooked a slice of ham. He ate it on bread and drank water, wishing he had thought to bring a bottle of whiskey. The next day, and the next, passed in solitude. On his third day here, he felt a presence, so he climbed into the rocks and waited.

An hour later two Seteks and two boys approached his camp. One of the Seteks carried a mag-pulsar. They rummaged around his camp for a short time, then spread out looking for him. It was the Setek he had sent to the hospital. He could tell by the ripped off ear.

Nicu wished he'd done whatever he was going to do, while the four were all together. Apart, they had an advantage.

He moved up the mountainside keeping out of view. He reached a wall of rock, climbed a short distance, and found a protected outcropping.

The four made their way to the rock face but kept their distance. They talked for a minute, and one of the boys took off, heading around to Nicu's left. The boy climbed a short distance up the rock wall, and when he stood to catch a peek, Nicu fired the Colt forty-five. The boy fell.

Those below began firing at Nicu. The mag-pulsar burned hole after hole in the rocks around him, but he was well sheltered.

It became quiet.

"You're a dead man! We can wait days . . . starve you out."

"I'm sure you can."

"Come down and we'll let you live."

He didn't reply; he knew they lied.

Nicu sat assessing his situation. He hadn't really thought this through. To escape, he'd have to climb and it would be dangerous. The rock wall towered several hundred feet above him and became more vertical the higher it got.

He decided he would climb after nightfall; the best route would be to work his way up and to his left. While more exposed, it was an easier climb.

Once the sun set and darkness overtook the mountain, Nicu set out. The going was slow, and the route treacherous. Every once in a while, one of the three would fire a shot in his direction, but none was close. He supposed they intended to keep him hunkered down in the rocks.

Nicu made his way to a somewhat level boulder field, but rocks and pebbles constantly shifted as he walked through them. He slipped, sending a small avalanche down the mountain.

That brought his adversaries running. The Setek fired the mag-pulsar, but the distance was too great for it to be effective. Two rifle shots narrowly missed him. A moment passed while Nicu reflected on his fate.

Three thunderous shots rang across the mountain. Shotgun blasts.

"You can come down now Nicu! You're safe."

He sighed, and made his way down, walking and sliding. When he got to the bottom and stood on solid ground, Jaelle stood next to the three dead boys. "Saved your ass, Nicu."

"You did. Thanks."

"I don't think you want to thank me." She held the mag-pulsar with her left hand. "These are worth a fortune. So, do I let you live, or kill you?"

"My choice?"

"No. Mine." She raised her right arm, pointing the shotgun at his chest.

"Pull that trigger, and it will be the last thing you ever pull," a woman's voice said.

Nicu was nearly laughing; he had never been the center of so much attention.

"He'll still be dead."

"You won't see him drop. Now, put the guns down."

Nicu recognized B's voice.

Jaelle dropped the guns and turned to face B.

B walked over. "You didn't see that coming, Jaelle. I followed you from town, 'cause you looked hungry. Nicu, we have work. Get the guns. All of them." She pointed the rifle at his chest. "Tie up the girl."

"What are you going to do with me?" said Jaelle.

"Nothing." She instructed Nicu to tie the shotgun around the girl's neck. "Just walk away, stay on the road."

After Jaelle left with her hands tied, Nicu said, "Why did you really follow me?"

"I want what you want, for different reasons."

"Money. What about me?"

"Go where you like. I'm taking the weapons." She now held a pistol on him.

"I can look you up."

She smiled and walked to her horse. "I hope you do." She led a horse back, never wavering the pistol's aim. "Tie the guns on the saddle."

Nicu tied the mag-pulsar and the two rifles to the saddle, the other tucked in her belt. "So long, pal."

She winked and rode away.

~

Two months later, B rode into Alamosa on a Moped. Nicu had moved into her house, believing she would never be back. She parked in front and honked. He stepped through the door and waved.

She walked to the door while Nicu slowly walked around the small scooter.

She came back out. "It's yours. Maybe I should have gotten you more. I appreciate all you did—looks homey."

He nodded. "Jaelle is still pissed at you."

"I saw her. She raised her shotgun at me. Didn't fire, as you can tell."

"Now what?"

"You can stay here."

"Keys?"

She tossed them to him.

He said, "I'll be back later. I have business."

She nodded and closed the door.

~

He drove the Moped to Lady Seltzer's ranch.

Bridgette met him at the door in tears. "Aunt Issa died."

"I'm sorry. Is there—"

"She died from natural causes. I'd like for you to say something graveside."

He leaned against a porch post and sagged. He removed his cap and closed his eyes. When he'd heard about Lady Seltzer helping the needy, he had knocked on her door. She'd given him food, clothes, and shelter; and initially she only asked that he carry his own weight in return.

The entire time he knew her, he witnessed her doing the same, time after time. He carried his load and the weight of a few others. Then she had demanded one unpleasant thing from him: she ordered him to bury an infant Setek. The infant had possessed Lady Seltzer's nose and blue eyes; no alien had blue eyes. He'd dug a hole and thrown the baby in, then went back to kill her. Wisely, he had turned and left the ranch instead. He knew she had done things unacceptable to most, and he had watched her require others to do things that were unprincipled. With no other work in Alamosa, he continued working for her off and on.

He was repulsed by her exploit—which he never forgave her for—and the deeds she exacted from those she saved; yet he also saw the immeasurable good she had done for those less fortunate.

Graveside, he would talk about how she gave, how she loved people, how she supported the town. He wouldn't address the other side.

He asked Bridgette who she left the ranch to.

"My brother, my cousin, and me."

~

Late that afternoon, over a hundred people from the town and countryside congregated at the Seltzer ranch. A grave had been dug in the family plot, and her casket rested on a platform attached to ropes.

Bridgette cried, her brother looked stoic, and her cousin looked bewildered. Nicu spoke kindly of Lady Seltzer, but inside he was furious. He left afterward and rode the moped to the sand dunes, hoping to find solace.

B had not shown up at the funeral.

That bothered him the most. Lady Seltzer had taken her in when she arrived alone in Alamosa, and had made her home, B's home. She had even given B a start, by giving her a computer.

He knew he could not face B right now. He had no idea what he would do if he did, but it would not be nice. Almost the whole town was there. She should have been there.

He patrolled Route 17.

The last month he had been ridding the road of gangs, for which Lady Seltzer paid him in food. Without thinking, he guarded the highway because he had to stay away from B and the Seltzer clan; he could not hide the disdain he felt for both. He had been there for a few hours when a rider on horseback approached.

"Hi." Bridgette said. "I had to get away. Everything came crashing in on me."

"Why are you here?" He glared at her.

"I thought we could talk." She sat on the ground in front of him. "You want to know where they hang out?"

"No."

"What has your ire?'

"You, your brother, your cousin . . . and B."

"We are her only family."

"And blood is thicker than—"

"You don't understand. She tried to right her wrongs— and don't accuse people you don't know anything about. Why B?"

"She wasn't there. Lady Seltzer gave her everything she has, and she couldn't bother to show up."

"She did give B a lot, and demanded even more in return. B wouldn't give Aunt Issa the child she wanted."

Nicu stabbed the ground with a stick. *Her too?*

"Ask her." She poked at the ground too. "Why did you work for my aunt?"

"She paid me. It's the only job I had."

"You have no pride."

"Unlike you?"

She almost stood to slap him, but then she relaxed and poked at the dwindling fire. "You could be right. A car's coming. Probably Johnny; you killed a couple of his boys."

Nicu killed the fire and walked away, looking up the road. "Come on."

She led the horse and fell in step with him. She looked at his back wondering why he was in no hurry.

The car turned off the road and stopped where the campfire had been, searchlights scanning the horizon.

Nicu, Bridgette, and the horse hid in a draw behind a sand dune. Shortly, the sound of the mufflerless car became louder, and it bounced across dunes, headlights showing the way, and searchlights panning in every direction.

"Go a ways down into the creek bed," Nicu told her. "And stay put. I'm going to take them out."

He lay on a dirt mound and aimed. He fired, the windshield exploded; he aimed and fired again.

The car stopped. Two men holding rifles got out and gazed into the desert. He fired again and again. They fell, and vehicle was Nicu's.

They walked over to the idling car. A Setek sitting in the passenger seat looked at Bridgette. "Help me, Bridge. I'm shot."

Nicu walked over to him and said, "God, her too?"

"Help me. I'm hit."

He fired. "You want the horse or car?" He glared at Bridgette. "Your aunt hoped I would kill you out here; now she leaves you the ranch. Well?"

She nodded toward the horse, then hastily mounted and spurred the horse towards the ranch without saying a word or looking back.

Nicu put the Moped in the back of the jeep and drove to town. He parked the jeep at Jaelle's place, and rode the Moped back to B's. When he got there, B was passed out; once again the empty Mason jar was on the floor next to her. He lifted her off the floor and put her on her bed, then sat at the table the rest of the night.

~

B staggered to the table and sat. "I missed you, Nicu. I thought you'd be mad that I sold the mag-gun."

"I would have sold it too, B. I'm sorry; I didn't understand. Bridgette—"

"Seltzer passed. Her influence over you is done. We move on."

"I didn't know she was at the center of your anger with me."

"She's dead. Move back in; your stuff is all still here."

"We're not all that good for each other."

"You alone keep me sober." She tried to laugh but grabbed her head. "And I alone keep you . . ." she leaned across the table and kissed Nicu on the lips, ". . . in tequila sunrise."

Memories

Maxwell Zwain

Where would we be without memories?
Who would we be without memories?
Memories are the stories that make up who we are.
They make up our lives, remembering those
we loved and lost.

Who are we without but a single memory?
Where in our lives would we be without a memory?
Memories can give us hope.

Hope to learn from past mistakes
and hope that we can better improve ourselves
in the future.

Without memories we would be lost.
A memory can be the light shining at the end
of a dark tunnel, guiding us.
Where would we be in our lives without our
memories?

One Last Score

Dusty Grein

I'm still not sure what went wrong; in fact, I don't remember much about last night at all. I'd like to blame God, or fate, or just bad damn luck; but I reckon the fault might lie some-wheres closer to home.

The train from Guaymas to Nogales was supposedly carryin' a shipment of gold—a tribute from the new Mexican Republic to the Governor of Arizona, or some such political nonsense.

Me and the boys, hell, we didn't care about nothin' but gettin' our hands on all that loot, and high-tailin' it south. We planned on sittin' on some sunny beach where the gold could be spent, the margaritas was sweet, and the senoritas was plentiful.

Bart Jonas and his cousin Dillon got the schedule off'n a Southern Pacific station master over at Tombstone, before they shot him and left his body for the buzzards.

The train was supposedly bein' guarded by a dozen rurales and at least one Mexican Federale, travelin' north with the gold. From what the boys heard, the third passenger car was actually converted to an armored transport for the safe.

The problems started when we derailed the damn train. Jim Bernard was our powder monkey, and he'd blown the tracks just north of Cibuta. The train derailed alright, but it was goin' faster than we thought, and it piled up end-over-end out there in the desert, among the sage and saguaros.

The Federale was killed outright, but the rurales turned out to be trained soldiers from the Mexican army, and they was a tough bunch of bastards. After a gunfight that seemed to last forever, me and Bart was the only two left standin'. Dillon and old Jim were layin' dead in the dirt, and all the Mexicans was either shot or they run off.

We found the safe layin' on its side, all banged up and dented. What with Jim bein' dead and all, it took over an hour for Bart to finally blast the hinges off of it, and he almost lost his left hand in the process. Once it was opened, it turned out the safe was stuffed plumb near full of 50 peso gold coins. We loaded our bags and dragged 'em back to the horses we'd left tied-off out in the hills; we mounted up and rode as hard as we could for the coast.

That was day before yesterday.

We rode them horses damn near into the dirt, and finally finished up in a little seaside fishin' town as the sun was comin' up. We found us an empty barn, and racked out.

Bart woke me near sundown, and we found our way to a little cantina near the wharf.

Wasn't hardly nobody there, 'cept a grizzled old barkeep, and an ugly painted-up senora who didn't speak no English.

I told Bart he should just pay with some of the copper pennies we had been savin' but he had to go and be a big shot. He flipped one of them big gold coins on the bar, and the keep's eyes damn near jumped outta his head.

We each grabbed a bottle of tequila and made our way over to the table where the whore was keepin' house. I do recall she got a little prettier with each drink, but that's about all I remember.

All I'd wanted was to head south, get my feet up, and live like a king, or at least a landed gentleman. That was before I woke up in this damn cell.

Now my head is poundin' and I'm alone in this dirty cage. I looked out the barred window a while ago, and I saw someone hanging by the neck from a scaffold. I think it's Bart, but I can't tell for sure.

I hope, if they're comin' for me next, they at least get a fresh rope.

I Was Always Afraid of Rabbits

Lynn White

"I was always afraid of rabbits"
said the purple dragon.
I knew it to be true.
I'd known him for a long time,
long before I became a witch
and took to the water
to watch over him.

It's the white ones he fears most
and they are mostly white ones
down here.
He won't eat them.

He used to eat fish
but now he is afraid to eat them
now he's seen them eating the rabbits.
They've eaten the fur off this one,
but he believes it was white
and believing is seeing
after all.

The fish have eaten everything
except for the head and eyes
the most fearsome parts
for the purple dragon.
It's found him now,
he pushes it away in panic
but it won't go,
it won't go.

It's covering his face,
taking it over
and getting ready
for the rest.

It won't go,
not unless I can grasp it,
and hold it
peel it off
take it away,
then bewitch them both.

First published in
With Painted Words, 2018

Again for the First Time

Sandi Hoover & Jim Tritten

Mark tapped the numbers into his phone and closed his eyes while it rang. They were now hundreds of miles apart, but he could still feel Eve clinging to him as he kissed her wet cheek before her flight.

Her shaky voice resounded in his memory, "I don't want to say goodbye. I love you; I can't believe love could be so deep, so fast. You touched my soul and renewed my life. I am so grateful."

A mechanical voice jarred him as it interrupted the unanswered ringing.

"THE NUMBER YOU HAVE CALLED HAS BEEN CHANGED, OR IS NO LONGER IN SERVICE. IF YOU THINK YOU HAVE RECEIVED THIS MESSAGE IN ERROR, PLEASE HANG UP AND DIAL AGAIN."

Must be a mistake.

He redialed; the unfeeling voice repeated the chilling statement.

Staring in disbelief, he dropped into the nearest chair.

Must've misread her printing.

He unfolded and looked once again at the Fiji Natewu Bay Resort's notepaper she'd used in lieu of a business card.

EVE JOHNSON, (917) 524- . . .

He compared the number he had dialed on his phone.

No, it's right. What the hell?

Mark rubbed his temples. He glowered at the phone and shouted. "We had a week of fun, fell in love, had terrific sex, and now I got a wrong number? Are you kidding me?"

He sat at the kitchen table in front of his uneaten breakfast, thinking as he held his coffee.

Doesn't make sense. Number not working. You can find anyone online.

He moved to the library, sat at his desk, and opened his laptop. He tapped out an email to the address Eve had written under her number and pushed Send. A quiet ding on his computer, and a rapid reply to his communication:

"PERMANENT ERROR. THIS IS AN AUTOMATICALLY GENERATED DELIVERY STATUS NOTIFICATION. DELIVERY TO THE FOLLOWING RECIPIENT FAILED PERMANENTLY."

Mark clenched his jaw. "Shit."

Okay, check Facebook. Everybody's on Facebook.

He typed every variation of Eve, then Johnson. Evie, Eva, Evita, Evelyn, Jonson, Johnston, Joinson. He found no one whose profile or photo came close.

LinkedIn. She's a professional; she'll be on there.

Mark hunted for Eve with the variations with no luck. He leaned back dumbfounded. Twitter, Instagram, YouTube, Google+, all gave similar results. His shoulders sagged. He picked up his cold coffee while he thought of why she would have given him bad contact information. Every reason made him shake his head.

Why?

Mark pondered the question then rose from his chair to look through the receipts from his trip. There was the hotel bill. He reached for his phone and started an international call.

"Natewu Bay Resort, how may I direct your call?"

"Reservations please."

"I'm sorry, but reservations does not open until 8:00 am. How can I help you?"

"This is Mark Adams; I was there three days ago . . . in Bungalow eight?"

A moment of silence then the clerk replied, "Ah yes, Mr. Adams, I see your stay in the computer. Was there a problem?"

"Yes. By the way, I didn't get your name."

"My name is Shanelle, how may I help you?"

"Shanelle, I took some photographs of the lady who was staying in bungalow nine, and I've misplaced her contact information. Could you possibly give me her email or phone number?"

"I'm very sorry Mr. Adams, but our resort has a strict privacy policy. We never reveal details about any of our guests, I'm sure you understand."

"I do, but she wanted a photo I took of her sailing, to show her husband. She wants them to buy that kind of a boat."

"I am sorry, Mr. Adams. I am afraid I am unable to provide you with any information."

"Can you at least confirm that her name is Eve Johnson?"

There was another moment of silence.

Shanelle whispered, "No, Mr. Adams, that's not her

name. Now really, that's all I can tell you."

Mark gritted his teeth, and hung up.

He closed the laptop and collapsed in his chair. He slammed his palms on his desk. "Shit."

~

Sitting back in the kitchen, Mark finished off a beer. He took a bite of his sandwich and held a third ice-cold can up to his forehead.

Why false information? Was she some sort of international thief?

Thinking over their conversation about her reason for being on Fiji, he remembered her comment about a medical conference. He considered scouring hospitals in New York City, but what would be the point? Her name wasn't Eve Johnson, and at this point, he didn't even know if she lived on the east coast, let alone in New York.

She lied to me. Who the hell is she?

Foam flew when he slammed the can down.

Mark threw himself into work. His return to his office the next day helped his strategy of keeping busy to avoid thinking about Eve. But thoughts intruded at inopportune times.

Why can't I get her out of my mind? She made her feelings so clear. Why doesn't she want to hear from me? Abusive ex-husband? Still married? Fearful of my reaction?

~

A month later Mark met up with Nathan, a friend from law school at Hawaii West, one of San Francisco's hangouts for singles.

"Hey Mark, you got plans for Thanksgiving?"

Mark winced. "No plans. Let me buy you a *Tecate* and maybe after a few we can talk about stuff."

"How's Tesla treating you? Still a new car every year?"

"I've been thinking about chucking it and getting away from this craziness."

Nathan's eyebrows went up. Mark offered no further explanation, staring at his beer instead.

Over a second *Tecate*, Mark pondered his drink and took a deep breath. "What would you think . . . no, what would you do, if you met a woman, had a short but intense relationship, and then learned everything she said was a lie?"

Nathan stared at Mark. "Huh, like you've never done that? Is this a rhetorical question or something serious I should understand? Do I need to put on my attorney hat?"

"It's a stupid question. She's disappeared. Even if I blew off her lying, I can't find her."

"Okay, I need to hear about this," Nathan said.

"It's a long story; feel free to fortify yourself."

Mark shared his story; meeting Eve in Fiji, and their week together.

Nathan looked at his friend, "Mark, it's time for you to put this affair behind you, and move on."

"I know, you're right, but I can't get her out of my head."

"Hey buddy; there're a million fish out there. Let's you and me go on the prowl. We never had any problem finding women and didn't care if they gave us their real name, did we?"

Mark shook his head.

Nathan asked, "Then, what do you want?"

"I wish I knew. It changes from day to day. When I remember how it felt when we were together, I want her, period. When I come to the end of our time and know it was a masquerade, I just want answers, so I can shut the book and walk away." Mark's pained expression said walking away would be hard.

"Okay buddy, if she means so much to you, why don't you hire a professional investigator? A female who looks like Scarlett Johansson, so even if she doesn't find this mystery woman, you haven't wasted your money."

"Nathan, you're not taking this seriously."

"Lighten up!"

"No, really—what would be the point of paying someone, if Eve doesn't want to be found?"

"A PI could find information where you can't."

"Okay, say this investigator finds her. Then what?" Mark pondered.

Yeah, then what?

~

Michelle entered the living room, her footsteps loudly resounding on the oak floor. Without furniture and numerous antique rugs muffling the clatter of shoes, the emptiness was startling.

"Steven, I . . . I won't forget." Tears filled her eyes, blurring the fireplace and adjacent windows.

How many winters we curled up here with a fire on chilly weekends. Reading together. Talking. Enjoying being close.

Sobbing, she grabbed a tissue.

Too many memories. Maybe another couple can build love in this place.

She gazed unseeing through windows overlooking a large park. The noise of cupboard doors elsewhere in the house brought her back to the duty at hand. She opened the doors on a cabinet between the fireplace and the window wall. Kneeling, she saw something at the rear of the bottom shelf.

The old, crumpled paper didn't want to unfold at first, but she insisted and then gasped as she read the title on the travel brochure she found.

"VISIT FIJI AND ENJOY A SOUTH SEAS PARADISE."

Her crying became a wail. Her sister, Kathleen, hurried around the corner and grabbed her. Michelle clung to Kathleen while her shoulders shook from crying.

As Michelle's emotion diminished, her sister handed her a fresh tissue and turned her toward the patio doors. "Let's go sit for a minute, and you can tell me what brought this on."

The summer's warmth and the beauty of the setting helped. Perched on the patio wall, she handed the paper to Kathleen.

"This is the brochure Steve and I looked at when we decided Fiji was perfect for our anniversary trip . . . before we knew about his illness. But that's not it. I haven't told anyone since I . . . I've tried not to think about it, but I . . . I can't leave the thought alone. This is killing me. I feel guilty when I think of it, and I can't stop thinking."

Michelle took a deep breath. "I met a man last year . . . much more than an affair . . . in Fiji." She leaned forward, hands between her knees, head bowed.

Kathleen said nothing but put her hand on her sister's back.

"Then I came home to find Steve had died. I've lived with this, and I can't stand it!"

"Don't you think you've suffered long enough?"

"Oh . . . I don't know." she stood and paced around the patio.

Kathleen stood up and opened her arms. Another hug opened the floodgate, and between tears, Michelle poured out the story of her week in Fiji, how she told Mark her name was Eve Johnson, and then had given him a made-up phone number and email.

~

As the months went by, Mark's suffering showed. His fashionable stubble grew into an unkempt beard, and let his hair get long, far beyond the norm. Lunches went from being business oriented, to lone forays to Hawaii West in North Beach, where he watched Sonia pour shots and dance behind the bar. Even a good-looking blonde didn't take his mind off Eve, or whatever her name really was.

His boss told him to take some time off and get his head screwed on straight. Mark's mind circled his pain again and again.

How could I have been so wrong?

Instead of easing, his pain grew.

Nathan joined him from time to time, watching Mark sink lower and lower. One Friday at happy hour, Sonia spoke up as the two old friends sat at the bar. "I'm sick and tired of listening to you crying in your beer. You, with the fuzzy face. Do you want this woman, or not?"

Stunned by this direct question, Mark looked at Sonia and his jaw dropped. "I want her."

"Well, then, why don't you do something to get her?"

Nathan added, "Yeah buddy, I've said it too. Get off your ass and do something!"

~

In late August, Mark hired a private eye. Nancy, a solidly-built retired Marine Corps investigator, laid out a plan to find Eve.

She contacted a friend in the Embassy guards at the American Consulate in Sydney, to find the medical conference Eve had supposedly attended. He provided her with the name of the conference, the local organizing host, and its web site.

Together, Mark and Nancy searched through the website, looking at photos from the conference.

"There she is!" Mark pointed out Eve to Nancy.

It wasn't a great shot, and they couldn't read her nametag, but Mark took comfort in at least validating the existence of his mystery woman.

Nancy said, "I think the way to get this woman's name

is to return to Fiji and do some snooping. A few greased palms here and there, and I can have her name, rank, and serial number."

"First, let me ask you a question. If you lied to a guy, made it impossible to find you, and then this guy contacts you anyway, what would your reaction be?"

"Hmmm. Depends. If I went to the trouble of erasing my trail, there would have to be a damn good reason. She married?"

"Widowed."

"You sure the husband is dead?"

Mark took a sharp breath. "That was my first guess; she's married and lied about her husband being dead."

"Wouldn't be the first time wifey got some on the side during a business trip."

Mark thought about this while he stared at the computer. "Even so . . . if she isn't in a healthy marriage, why doesn't she just leave him? She told me she loved me."

"Listen, Mark. The bottom line is she didn't want to be found. If someone came after me when I had made that as difficult as I could, well . . ."

"Well what??

"Well, I'd either send him packing, or start making plans to get rid of hubby."

Mark thought hard before he admitted, "I can forgive anything, if only I can see her once more."

"If you hope to get anywhere with this woman, you'd better clean up your act." Nancy shook her head. "A shower and change of clothes will be a good start."

~

In her Manhattan apartment, Michelle paused over the computer keyboard.

Okay, make a decision. Contact Mark and admit what I did? Is my hesitation in writing, telling me to let it go? That week was as wonderful as anything Steven and I ever had. It reminded me of early times in our marriage. Discovering mutual interests. The excitement of compatibility. Awesome sex. I needed what we had, and really did love him for it.

The paper with Tesla's address was sitting on her desk, propped against a figurine of Buddha. Using Google to find Mark had been one of the first things she'd done after getting settled in the apartment. She glanced at the paper.

Well, Mark, do you want to hear from me? I've started this letter twice in the last month . . . and deleted it every time. How do I begin? What can I say so you understand—before you throw it away?

She stood and paced, down the hall and back, then grabbed her purse and left the apartment.

The elevator took her to the ground floor as she stabbed at her phone. "Kathleen? Can you meet me at the park? At the carousel? Thanks, I'll see you there."

Thank God for my sister.

~

It was a beautiful late summer Saturday, but Michelle hardly noticed. Kathleen bounded to her feet from a bench near the carousel and waved. After an intense hug, she said, "Okay, what's going on? You sounded stressed, and you look like you haven't slept for days."

Michelle sat. "Make that almost a year of poor sleeping."

"Darling, you're looking anorexic."

"Oh Kathy, I still don't know what to do. The combo of guilt over Steven's death, and guilt over lying to Mark is weighing on me.

"Tell me while we walk."

"Did Mark also think we had something special? If he was as much in love with me as he said, before we left Fiji . . . when he figured out I lied, he would've been hurt, badly. I didn't think very far ahead during our week. I got caught up in the speed and intensity of our relationship, and couldn't back out. I didn't want to. I didn't expect our connection, or the happiness of living and loving again."

"Sis, you are a head case. First, you bury yourself in guilt because you cheated on Steve—who would have encouraged you had he known. Now you're wrapped in more guilt over the guy you cheated with. Did you write to him?"

"No. I've started several letters, but deleted all of them."

"Well, I can't write the words for you, but you need to get this off your chest before you make yourself even sicker. Come on; act on your feelings. I told you that months ago. Go home and tell this guy how you feel, how you felt, and what the hell has been going on."

Back in her apartment, Michelle sat down, rubbed her right shoulder, cramping from tension, and started to type yet again.

This time, I'm mailing it.

~

In Palo Alto, Mark puzzled over the envelope's return address.

Ms. Michelle Williams

A name he didn't recognize and a downtown Manhattan street address with postmark on September twentieth. Not the typical solicitation letter. He sometimes got donation requests, but a handwritten envelope was different.

The writing appeared vaguely familiar as he looked at the weighty envelope. It had been sent to the Tesla Corporation address, but marked for his attention.

Letters were unusual in his business life, so he was intrigued as he opened and read.

Dear Mark,

By now you must know Eve lied to you, and there is no way I can tell you how sorry I am. In those first few minutes of meeting, I only thought to keep my real self, and that unknown woman you met, separate.

Shaking as he realized he was holding the answers to questions he'd pondered for almost a year, Mark refolded the letter after reading those first sentences.

This open floor plan is good for working together, but not for privacy. Waited this long for answers. What timing. Nancy is flying to Fiji tonight.

He grabbed a cup of coffee, and took it and the letter with him to a nearby park.

Life was complicated with Steve, and I just wanted a simple evening to enjoy a lighthearted conversation.

I KNEW HE WAS DYING BUT WATCHING IT HAPPEN BY DEGREES WAS TOO PAINFUL.

YOU KEPT ME FROM THINKING ABOUT IT WHILE WE WERE TOGETHER, BUT I KNEW IT WOULD ONLY BE FOR ONE WEEK.

The letter went on, recounting her arrival in the States to find her husband had died during her flight home from Fiji—triggering unending guilt. She touched on her months filled with grieving and her decision to sell her home and escape the painful memories. She regretted the time lost by not contacting him sooner to confess her deception, so he wouldn't think it was somehow his fault. She apologized for any emotional distress she caused and would understand if she never heard from him.

I HAD TO LET YOU KNOW THERE WAS NOTHING DISHONEST ABOUT MY FEELINGS AND ACTIONS DURING OUR DAYS AND NIGHTS. THE HAPPINESS AND JOY WE SHARED WERE REAL, AND I KNOW BEGINNING A RELATIONSHIP WITH A LIE WAS WRONG. I DIDN'T EXPECT TO HAVE MORE THAN AN EVENING'S DRINK AND DINNER.

PLEASE FORGIVE ME AND BELIEVE I LOVED YOU IN FIJI, AND AM WRITING THIS BECAUSE I LOVE YOU STILL.

MICHELLE.

Her contact information was below her signature.

Mark sat bundled in his coat, the cold of the bench seeping into his seat and thighs. He needed the benediction of warmth; September in the Bay Area was never warm.

He reread the last lines of her letter, remembering

conversations, savoring the laughter they had shared over comedians they liked, finding common interests, books they had both read and enjoyed discussing.

Mark stuffed the letter into the envelope as he weighed Michelle's explanation. He called his secretary, said he was not feeling well and was going home. He shoved his hands in his pockets and started walking, a habit he had when wrestling a problem's details.

She's right; I don't want a relationship with someone who could live a lie. Michelle, not Eve. She should have trusted me and let me understand who she really was. Her past year must've been hell. It's been hell for me too. Gotta call Nancy.

Mark got her voice mail. "Nancy, cancel the trip to Fiji. Call me later." He quickly sent her a text and an email.

A second call was to his friend. "Hey, Nathan. Can I buy you a drink and get your opinion on Act Two of my melodrama? I've heard from my mystery woman. Are you curious?"

~

After they ordered beers, Nathan said, "You got me here with a teaser about your female from Fiji reappearing after a year. What's happened?"

Mark started to give him a brief recap of Michelle's letter, then changed his mind. "Here, read it for yourself."

Nathan kept a poker face through most of the letter, but appeared pained as he neared the end. He finished and scrutinized Mark. "Well, what are you going to do?"

"I don't know. I'm not sure what I feel. First anger, now . . ."

"Do you want to see, uh, *Michelle* again?" Nathan asked.

"I don't know! If I don't care about her, why am I so unhappy about what she did? And why do I feel so damned defensive?"

Nathan said nothing, simply watched Mark.

"A piece of me is relieved to hear from her, and have her say she's sorry she hurt me. Damn right, I was hurt; I still am. It's some consolation she's hurting too, and that sounds selfish and petty . . . but I'd comfort her if she were here. She had a rough time when she got home."

"Conflicted much?" Nathan interjected as Mark took a breath. "Look, Mark. Try our old flip-a-coin trick. Heads you go see her, tails you tear up the letter. If you get tails and say 'I'll try for two out of three,' then you've made your decision."

Mark chuckled remembering the times they'd used that in law school, and it had usually landed them in trouble. "But seriously, I'm not sure what's the best thing to do."

Nathan glared at Mark. "You're kidding, aren't you? It's written all over you, and in everything you say. You've got to see what you two have left, if nothing else. Then you'll know what to do. Go see her."

~

Mark stood opposite Michelle's apartment building debating what to do.

How will we begin again? Should I have called first? Does Michelle make love with as much abandon as Eve?

His head buzzed as he leaned on a tree trunk.

Standing here like a frightened schoolboy is ridiculous.

He walked down the block and around the corner. Finding

his stride, and his usual comfort in walking to solve a problem, he kept on for another block, on around another corner, and more. He discovered a pocket park where reds and golds of oaks shimmered in the afternoon light. He removed his too warm leather jacket—and felt his phone in the pocket.

The way to find out if she's home is to call her. Then we can either meet somewhere, or I can go to her door.

He called the number from her letter, and almost hung up on the first ring when he wasn't sure what he'd say if she answered. At the fourth ring, he heard Michelle's recorded voice, recognizable despite her severe tone.

"HELLO, IF YOU'RE A TELEMARKETER, YOU CAN HANG UP. OTHERWISE PLEASE LEAVE YOUR NAME, NUMBER, AND A SHORT MESSAGE."

Mark wavered, then said in a sociable voice, "Hello, Michelle, if I may call you Michelle, instead of Eve. Shakespeare would tell you I'm worse than a telemarketer, but we decided once upon a time that lawyers weren't so bad." His hand holding the phone shook.

He heard a gasp of surprise on her end, as she picked up the phone, and silence for a moment before he heard sobs.

"Hey, that was supposed to be an ice breaker, not a heartbreaker."

In his ear, a squelched sob ended with a hiccup and an almost giggle.

"That's better Eee . . . uh . . . Michelle. It's hard to get used to that name. I should've given you some warning, but I was afraid—don't ask me why."

"Oh, Mark." Michelle sniffled. "I hoped you would forgive my bungled start to our relationship. You were supposed to be company for one evening—just a drink, and maybe a meal. Really, I hadn't even thought that far ahead. You changed my world—brought joy and love back."

"I'll take that as a compliment."

"It's intended as honesty, not flattery," Michelle said. "The hell I've been through for months has taught me that lesson well. Never anything less than the truth will do."

"Continuing in that vein, how do we take the next step in creating a relationship based on our real selves, assuming you wish to renew or begin something?" Mark's voice rose a little—straining to sound comfortable with any answer.

Through another sniffle, Michelle managed a small laugh. "That makes me happier than I've been in a long time."

"God, it's wonderful to hear your voice again."

"Mark, we had something extraordinary, or I wouldn't have written my lengthy explanation."

"We did, or rather . . . we do, don't we?" Mark waited as the silence seemed like it would never end.

"Yes. Yes." This time both of them were silent until Michelle added, "Just the prospect of building something with you means while we don't erase the past, we can set it aside."

Mark answered, "I'm not sure I want to set aside everything. I found someone to replace Eve." He heard the sudden intake of air being cut short. "I decided I had to meet Michelle."

Her ripple of happy laughter was one he recognized.

"You're right; there are some things we remember vividly. Where should we meet? Halfway? Not Texas, perhaps Santa Fe?"

He leaped to his feet. "I'd like to not let months pass before we see if we still recognize one another. Can we meet sooner rather than later? I was wondering if you have a favorite restaurant near Soho where we could get a reservation this evening."

"What?" Michelle's voice was an octave higher than normal. "Are you in Manhattan?"

"Stranger things have happened than a coincidence in locations. Pick the time and place, and I'll be there. I hope you recognize me, since I don't have a carnation for my lapel. Actually, I don't even have lapels. Just tell me where to show up."

Laughing happily, Michelle said she would be at *Osteria Morini* in an hour.

"Really? You're going to make me wait that long?"

"Mark, I need a shower first."

"I understand; I was reminded about grooming recently."

After they hung up. Mark Googled the address for the Italian restaurant, and the nearest florist. Neither was very far. He walked, humming to himself, smiling all the way.

~

Michelle immediately called Kathleen and, even though she got voice mail, shared her feelings. "Mark's in town, and we're getting together for dinner." She stopped talking to laugh aloud. "I'm acting like a schoolgirl. I'm so excited! I think we have a chance. Thank you for your insistence I let him know the whole story."

Instead of showering, she sat on her bed and remembered walking on Fiji's beach, and then day-dreamed about a trip with Mark to a new place to create memories together.

Am I trying too hard? Oh shit! What am I going to wear? The Osteria is sorta casual. Not this, or this. Just the New York black uniform? Not that. I don't want to look like I'm in mourning.

Michelle leafed through her clothes in a frenzy, trying to make a decision. She finally chose a favorite pair of gray leggings, with black, almost knee-high boots, and a classic sweater in rust to highlight her hair, shaped enough to show off her figure. She spent a few minutes adding some eyeshadow.

Enough is enough. No more about how I look. How does he look? Have I exaggerated his incredible looks? Will we still be attracted to one another? Was it simply Fiji or something more? Time to find out.

She threw a stole in grays, rusts, and blues over her shoulders, grabbed her purse, locked the door, and strode down the street toward the restaurant.

She got to the Osteria Morini sooner than anticipated, before the hour passed. She was greeted as a favorite customer.

"Ah, good evening Ms. Michelle, are you expecting your sister tonight?" the young maitre'd inquired as she entered.

"No Tony, I have a date coming. May I have a quiet table toward the back?"

"But of course. Let me seat you. What is the name I should expect?"

"Mark Adams." She smiled and added, "He's tall . . . incredibly handsome . . . and you keep your hands off him."

Tony put a finger to his lips. "Aah, of course. I am pleased for you, Ms. Michelle. Would you like a martini while you wait?"

Michelle nodded as Tony pushed in her chair.

Did I imagine Tony radiating good vibes as he went to the bar?

She texted her sister she had arrived and felt her cheeks warm. Not waiting for Kathleen's response, she turned off her phone.

Her well-chilled martini arrived in short order. She casually glanced at her watch. If he was going to stand her up, she didn't want to know yet. Still a few minutes before he was late. Another sip of martini to give her hands something to do.

Why am I so nervous? I've known this man—intimately in fact. That's not true. We were intimate, but we didn't have time to get to know one another intimately. I want to know details. Is he punctual? I don't know. Would he let me know if he were going to be late? Shit, my phone's off!

Michelle was looking down, fumbling in her purse for her phone when she was startled by a voice that raised goosebumps.

"You are more beautiful than I remembered. The name Michelle fits you—graceful and just a little exotic, like these." He laid a single stem of perfect white Phalaenopsis orchids on the table. "It's nice to meet you again, for the first time, Ms. Williams."

Sending Thoughts Out Into The Universe

Michelle Murray

Sending thoughts out
into the universe,
of light,
love, family.

Sending thoughts out
to people I thought I would see again,
others who have crossed my path,
friends who have come and gone
on their own journey.

Sending thoughts out
into the universe,
to family who have passed away;
spirits who have come and gone
from this place.

Sending thoughts out
into the universe,
that on a cold dark night,
there is still light, there is still hope,
there is still love.

Somewhere out there,
someone is thinking of you;
they are
sending thoughts out
into the universe.

Release

Mandy Melanson

I hate the pain on Anna's face. It distorts her features. Her tears escape to the ground. A tiny puddle of false hopes and broken promises. She's probably thinking about *him*. "Don't worry, I took care of him. He won't hurt you, again." Her skin is like velvet under my touch.

I don't blame her for running; I must have startled her. A person can only be hurt so many times before they begin to expect it. It's natural to trust less and question more. "Stop," I yell. She must not be able to hear me. We tumble to the ground as I try to wrap her up and comfort her.

Her words hurt, but I know that I'm not what she says. It's my job to make her feel better—to release her from the pain he put her through. I will not fail—not again.

She bites at my hand as I hold the rag over her nose. Her nails claw at my face.

I think I see pieces of my skin underneath the chipped black nail polish. A drop of my blood falls on her skin. "Trust me. It won't hurt anymore . . ." I pull her up into my arms. "Sleep, my love. You're safe now. You'll stay with me."

Doll Eyes

Faith Maria Brody

The first thing that I noticed were the eyes. She had such visibly wanting eyes, as if she was staring right into me, asking me for something. I shook my head to myself, pulling myself away. It was silly. She was a doll. Her eyes were no more real than the Barbies I owned when I was growing up, leaving them in clumps, scattered on my bedroom floor.

"Isn't she a beauty?" The owner asked me, an older woman of around fifty, maybe sixty if I looked a little harder. It was hard to tell. She did a good job covering herself with makeup.

I nodded. "Very realistic," I added.

"Quite a bargain too at only $160. You don't see too many Madame BoJeanes anymore. She's a rarity."

"I've never even heard of her."

"Are you a collector?"

I shrugged. There were things gathering dust at home, but it wasn't as if I liked one thing more than another. There were things that I had, owned, coveted.

"I'm visiting," I said. "Sort of."

It was true that I wasn't from around here. Todd and I were in town trying to figure out what to do with my mother. She was old, had grown old real fast before I had the chance to realize it. We spent a while researching facilities that specialized in dementia, needing a place that could provide more help than I was able to give to her.

"Is that you, Barbara?" she would call out to me, sensing me in her presence.

Sometimes I would humor her, pretending that yes, I was my deceased sister that she was so fond of. But most of the time I told her the truth.

"No, Mom, it's just me. It's Tammy."

If I was Barbara, then I received a hug and an "I missed you". If I stayed me, then I got nothing or I got harassed.

So yes, I was just visiting.

"Family here?" she asked.

I shook my head.

"Vernon is a real fun town," the owner said, this time holding her hand out to me. "My name's Angie. It sure is nice to meet you."

I shook her hand, noticing her pressed on pink nails. Her ring fingers had little jewels on them.

"Same," I nodded.

"Take your time. Look around. You won't bother me."

Angie reached into a drawer and pulled out a Chinese food menu. I wondered if Todd was finished up with his work calls in the hotel business center so that we could eat soon too. Vernon was a "neat town" as Angie had mentioned to me, but it was tiny, and a bit off the grid.

Angie's doll shop, or museum, as she had grandly noted in a bright marquee, was located inside of an old movie theater on the town's main street. It was a great use of an old space, which is what originally caught my eye when I came wandering. The ticket booth had even caught me off guard at first, where a life size doll dressed in an old movie theater worker uniform sat propped up in the window, challenging my vision. It was the most interesting display I'd seen on a street containing a simple florist, diner, a handful of small shops, and an ice cream stand.

And so I entered, the lobby walls cluttered with beady, little eyes. A poster that read, The History of Dolls, was taped up to my left. It was obviously homemade, but provided with an interesting time line of the Ginnys and the Alexanders. I was in the shop for an hour, maybe two when I finally met with Angie, after observing the Madame Bo Jeane.

I felt transfixed by a little girl doll pushing a pram with a baby doll inside of it when I felt a tug at my shoulder.

"There you are," The smug voice of my husband startled me. Todd. "What are you doing in this cheesy place?"

I looked for evidence of Angie feeling insulted, but she was busy twirling her lo mein around a fork. Occupied.

"I needed something to do," I told him. "You were working."

"Did you check out Fern Valley?"

"Yes, it seems plenty suitable for my mother."

"I don't like this place."

"I didn't think you would."

Todd grabbed me by the wrist and pulled me away from the doll and her pram. For a moment, I thought I heard the baby cry.

"Come back again, now," Angie said on my way out.

The marquee lights glittered in the magic hour of the sky.

~

epsos.de

When Todd's hot roast beef arrived, he complained that there was too much gravy and had it sent back. I stared out the window onto the streets of Vernon. People strolled about, but not much. Would I be able to let my mother live in a town as quiet as this? Would I visit her? She would continue to miss Barbara. I missed her too.

When we were younger, we played in the attic of the house. We had matching dolls that wore Victorian style white nightgowns and little matching night caps. Mom could never afford those pricey American Girl style dolls, but we pretended that our dolls were them anyhow, and then pretended that we were the dolls. We took turns brushing each other's hair. Sometimes we pretended we were helpless babies. Barbara fed me from a bottle.

"I can't wait to get back to the city," said Todd. "Look at this food."

I was pushing my salad around my plate.

"I'm sorry you don't like it."

The waitress was one of those career waitresses. She stopped by with some more water.

"Anything else?" she asked in her thick, smoke-accented voice.

"I'm all finished," I told her.

When she cleared my plate, I noticed my placemat was one of those advertisements for local businesses around the area. The Fern Valley Retirement Home was listed there, as was The Doll Museum. Then I saw something else.

"Hey, Todd..."

"What?"

"Look."

I pointed to a missing girl ad. She was young, a teenager with big, brown eyes and a cheerleader's smile.

"It's a shame," he said.

"She reminds me of Barbara."

Whenever I did something like this, Todd didn't know what to say or how to act. Barbara went missing when we were tweens, assumed dead. She had those big brown eyes where mine were big but sad and blue. She had that giant smile where mine was almost nonexistent. It made sense why my mother didn't want to be around me. I should have been the one to go missing.

"I said it's a shame, Tammy. It happens a lot, though. Maybe they will find this girl."

Our waitress returned with our check.

"Has she been gone long?" I asked her.

"Hmmm?" I caught her off guard. "Oh, her. The Gibbons' girl. It's been about two weeks. Such a shame."

Such a shame. Well, that's all they could say when Barbara disappeared too. Such a shame.

~

My dreams that night were twisted thoughts about Barbara and the Gibbons' girl. I walked down the main street of Vernon, when I saw the doll museum, only it was still a movie theatre. The Gibbons' girl worked as the ticket taker. She smiled at me.

"Such a shame all the good films are sold out today."

"It's okay," I told her. "I'm only here to meet my sister."

She gestured to go on inside.

When I walked in through the front door, Barbara was waiting for me at a front counter, dressed like the dolls we owned when we were younger. Her back was to me.

"Barbara," I murmured.

"Tammy..."

Todd woke me up, shaking me.

"You're sweating," he said.

"I'm fine."

"We need to sign the contract for your mother tomorrow."

"Is that why you woke me up?"

"No, but it's on my mind."

"Fine, yes. You won't have to help take care of her anymore."

"It's not just for me. Soon you'll feel better too."

But what he really meant was if I didn't have to take care of her then I could be more focused on him. Todd wanted a wife who could shine, someone who could show up at work parties and look great in a slim black dress with fresh, blow dried hair and natural makeup. Someone who loved Pottery Barn and decorating and crafting clever little cocktails. Not me. I worried and I thought too much. I hated yoga and wine always made me too tired. We were a classic tale—the longer we were married the more I wondered why we had done it. I think he wanted to save me, but was disappointed to find out that I wasn't worth the saving.

"I'm going to step out for some air. You can go back to bed. I won't be long."

"Suit yourself. I'm not oversleeping and missing the breakfast part of bed and breakfast again."

He turned over onto his stomach, wrapped up in the thick comforter of the Dahlia room, the room I picked out for our comfort. I stepped out onto the balcony, overlooking Vernon. Not a single light was lit in the town below.

~

"You're back," Angie's face had the warmth of a television grandmother. Momentarily, I thought she might offer me a homemade cookie, but then noticed her convenience store slushie and breakfast burrito instead.

"I wanted to tour the place again," I told her. "It's quite fascinating. My husband is taking care of some paperwork that might be a while, so I have the time."

"People always say they never see the same things twice when they are here."

That morning, I signed everything that I needed to move my mother into Fern Valley, where she would receive around the clock care, top quality meals, a private nurse, beauty services, everything. I could visit her if I wanted to. If I wanted to.

"Did you want to see Madame BoJeane again?"

"No, thank you," I said. "I'll be around."

I walked toward the beginning hallway.

"Well," Angie began, "She misses you."

I turned my head to see Angie holding Madame BeJeane, propped up on her desk with her. She held the little doll's hand up into a wave toward me. I waved back.

Goodbye, I thought. *Goodbye.*

~

I decided to head en route to an upper floor, one I did not have a chance to previously see. I was above where the movie screen would have been, where the silent screen film stars were once the most exciting illusions to pass through Vernon. What was it like to grow up in a town like this, to live with this main street among the diner patrons and the old timers, the Woolworths crowd and the chain smoking waitresses?

I let my fingers run through the Rapunzel-like hair of a little girl doll with large, black eyes. She started into me. Why were these dolls always so young?

"Because no one wants to take care of an old lady", I said to myself, thinking of my mother. Would she like her new home? Who was I kidding? She wouldn't even know the difference.

I reached into my purse to grab my phone, seeing if Todd had messaged me at all. He planned to work all day again. We made plans to have a romantic dinner at one of the only nice restaurants in the area before wrapping up and heading home in the morning. No Todd. It wasn't unlike him.

He wasn't a sociopath. He didn't beat me, no, but do you need to do those things to qualify as a bad guy? A year before the visit to Vernon, my mother's health severely deteriorated. It's when she really began to think of me as Barbara, to wish that I was maybe. I spent a lot of time with her before temporarily moving her in with us.

Todd couldn't handle it. There were doctors' visits and phone calls from the neighbors or the police whenever she wandered into their homes by accident. I cried a lot, but tried not to in front of him.

"There are homes for people like her," he would always tell me. "People who are better suited to take care of her."

Because you don't want to be involved. Because you don't really care.

At one of his work parties, I stood in a corner most of the evening, hovering over my glass of wine.

"You're Tammy, aren't you? Todd's wife?" a dull looking blonde approached me. She wore a plain black dress and flats. She laughed at Todd's tasteless jokes with carefully curated laughter.

I managed a small smile and we shook hands.

"I'm Veronica. I do all of the marketing for Todd's projects. We work very closely together. It's so nice to meet you."

The way that she said it told me that she meant that it wasn't. There was no doubt that her and Todd were together, that they made fun of me, laughed about me, didn't understand me.

"She's not even pretty, Todd. I don't get it."

"Tammy, you aren't around. If you weren't around, it wouldn't have happened."

So we decided to put my mother in Fern Valley. For our relationship. And now he couldn't stop working.

~

I still hadn't heard from Todd. It was getting late. I figured I would head to the inn and maybe order some take out for myself. I approached the staircase when I noticed something I didn't see from before. Angie's words from earlier echoed in my mind.

People always say they never see the same things twice when they are here.

They were near the little girl doll with the Rapunzel hair, two identical dolls like sisters, with old fashioned night-gowns and matching night caps. They looked so much like the dolls of my childhood.

"Barbara," I whispered before everything went black and dark, like the end of a movie.

~

There were no sounds when I woke up. I looked around, trying to place where I was. My head rested beneath a soft pillow, but I wasn't in my bed from the inn. The mattress was very rough and flat. A frilly pink blanket was thrown nearby.

"Hush little baby, don't you cry," a woman's voice softly began to sing a familiar lullaby.

Why can't I see anything? I wondered.

When I looked to the sides, I saw that I was encased inside of the bed somehow. There were walls built around the mattress.

"Mama's gonna buy you a mockingbird."

I'll call Todd, I thought, reaching for my purse, before realizing that it was not in the bed with me. I touched the skin of my left arm. It was a warm, normal temperature. It didn't feel funny. I was a little tired. The last thing that I remembered was seeing those dolls from my childhood.

I flashed to a moment from when Barbara and I were kids. My mother had taken us to the beach for the day. We had our dolls sprawled out on the ratty beach blankets, taking in the sun with us, getting sand in their hair, just like us. She was laughing so much. She was such a happy kid with an effervescent laugh.

Back to now. It was a doll museum. And those dolls were cheaply made. I'm sure they could have been other copies of the dolls. It's just that they startled me so much. Did I fall? Or pass out because of the dolls? Is that what happened?

"And if that mockingbird don't sing..."

Get up, Tammy, I told myself. You need to get up.

My shoulders ached and my bones felt tired. It was easy to just lay down and die. Was Todd even worried? I pictured him eating dinner with Veronica, in our semi-classy restaurant. She was laughing the whole time, trying to impress him because his wife is such a downer.

Get up. Do it for Barbara.

Weird things couldn't happen to both children in a family. I tried to convince myself of this, although I did read a story once where one sister went missing and then a few years later another did end up dying from a rare form of cancer. It was tragic, but not weird. One sister going missing and then another being trapped in a large, strange bed was definitely weird. Eventually, even if Todd was with Veronica, he would have to notice I was missing and do something about it. Even if he hated me. If I live, I could be on Unsolved Mysteries or something similar. I could become a meme.

I stopped myself from laughing. Robert Stack was dead and memes were for the young.

"Mama's gonna buy you a wedding ring."

Get the fuck up.

I lifted myself up, from the waist first, a wash of heaviness and groggy pain falling through my body. Once up, I realized it was not a bed with walls, but a cradle, a massive white cradle for adults.

Or life size dolls.

I crawled over to the side of the cradle and carefully peered over the edge. Angie was sitting in a rocking chair, holding Madame BoJeane in her arms. She was singing to her. We were in a nursery. A life-size pram was by the door. A closet held little girl dresses in chiffon, polka dot and lace. Next to my cradle were several smaller cradles. Each cradle had a doll inside of it, tucked away cozily, sleeping.

"Okay, Madame, let's see how your new friend is doing."

Angie stepped out of her rocking chair, still holding the little doll in her arms like an infant. She made her way over to the bed.

"Well, hello," she said. "I see that you are awake."

I stood, my eyes staring.

"You like it so much here," she continued. "Wouldn't you like to stay?"

"I-I- have a family."

"That's not what you said before."

"My mother—"

"She doesn't need you anymore."

Angie placed Madame Bo Jeane into a nearby cradle, neatly tucking the little doll inside.

She kissed her lightly on the forehead. A tiny smudge of lipstick was left.

Angie then extended a hand out to me.

"Come on out."

Her hand was warm and soft. She was right. My mother didn't need me anymore. She didn't even know who I was, where I was.

"People think dolls are just for little kids," Angie said. "It's just not true, though."

I nodded.

"I never could have my own babies, either. Now I've got this whole nursery."

"It's beautiful."

Barbara would have liked it—the story, the place. Everything. She would have laughed about it.

"Have a seat," she gestured to her rocking chair. "I'll tell you what you need to know."

~

Todd was angry that I missed dinner. He didn't understand that I lost my phone in the doll museum and fainted. I explained how Angie was so kind to me, how she let me rest until I felt better.

"She had a spare bed upstairs, Todd. I didn't even think to call the inn to tell you. I just wanted to rest."

"When we get back home, you need to figure out what to do. It's time you went back to work, time you took more interest in my work friends," Todd said.

"Like who? Veronica?"

"That's been over, Tammy."

"It should never have started."

I stared at Todd, right in his face. He had nothing to say back to me this time.

"I want to stop at the doll museum one last time before we leave, and I'd like you to come with me."

"That weird place?"

"Maybe Angie found my phone."

"Fine."

Angie told me that she was always looking for new dolls. She went to estate sales, thrift stores, and bought some online. Others were special, though. Some she had to seek out. Some she found and had immediate attachments with. She knew she was in need of a new doll for the collection the first time that she met me.

"I feel a connection with you, Tammy. Did something happen in your life?"

I nodded.

"This can be a healing place," Angie said. "All these babies—no one else wanted them. I take good care of them, though."

The baby dolls slept peacefully in their cradles. The fashion dolls had perfectly brushed hair. Each doll under Angie's care had manicured nails, matching shoes, long lashes, a place in the world.

Did I want to stay in Vernon? I felt a sense of urgency to get home.

"I can't stay, but I think I can help you," I told her before I left that evening.

We hugged and I let her know I would stop by before I left for home.

"And Todd?" I asked.

"What?"

"Fern Valley isn't happening. It's too far. I want my mother to stay with us. I know you don't like it, but that's not for you to decide."

"We already signed the papers".

"We can un-sign them".

"I don't know what's wrong with you today. Too much time away from home I guess. Let's go." He grabbed my wrist for the last time.

~

The day that Barbara disappeared was the only time she and I had an argument. She wanted to take both twin dolls with her on a bike ride.

"It's so nice out, Tammy! I want to put them in my bike basket and go."

"No. One of them is mine."

"You come too, then."

"No. I want to stay here with Mom."

"Mom isn't even doing anything," she said, looking off into the living room.

Our mother was sitting on the sofa, watching her soaps and drinking a glass of wine. It was her day off from work.

"I was hoping she would want to spend time with me," I said quietly.

Barbara shrugged.

"I'm going out without you. And the dolls."

After that, she was gone, like a flicker of dust in the air. We never saw her again.

~

"You have a safe trip back," Angie said, before taking a sip from her slushie.

"I will."

"Fern Valley isn't all it's cracked up to be. Anyway, nothing compares to a daughter's love."

I managed a small smile, knowing I made the right decision.

I turned to Todd. He could say whatever he wanted, but the decision was made. My mother was staying with me, not several hours away.

"And you're good with everything?" I asked Angie.

"Don't you worry, sweetie pie. He'll be well taken care of here."

"Well then," I said. "Goodbye, Todd."

His face was in a permanent smile now, frat boy looks compared to a Ken doll. I had him placed up on a shelf near Angie's post, so she could always keep a watchful eye on him.

I held my hand out to Angie. She placed her hand in mine, a firm grip, knowing I wouldn't be back. It was easy enough to say that Todd decided to leave me after I decided not to place my mother in Fern Valley. People who knew him would believe it.

I almost believed it was true as I left the doll museum. As I left, I said a quick prayer that the Gibbons' girl would be found soon. Then I turned to make sure that the life size doll in the ticket booth didn't have her eyes on me.

She did.

Originally Published by Quail Bell Magazine,

The Unreal fiction, 01-09-2018

Smile

Lynn White

It was the purr she heard first,
so loud it was almost a growl.
But a dog up a tree?
No, she knew that would be mad!
So she wasn't surprised to see a cat
when she looked up
and wasn't surprised to see it smiling.
She expected it to be happy with so loud a purr.
You must be pleased to see me, she thought,
watching it stretch and sleepily curl.

She felt sleepy too and curled like the cat.
And they dreamed smiley dreams.
And then she heard a crash as the branches broke
and the cat landed heavily in her lap.
She was bruised, battered, broken.

Then she woke to find
the cat had disappeared.
Only the smile remained.
And that weighed nothing at all.

Shaken, and Stirred

Dusty Grein

What a difference 24 hours could make.

The trip to Peru had started out as just another mission. My job was to infiltrate Presidente Caxtone's palace and find the missing diamonds. We knew he had arranged to have them stolen. The intel I had been given by my handlers had pointed to a low-level computer specialist, one Tereza Sanchella, as the best possible way in.

I had followed her to a small bar on the outskirts of the city of Santa Maria. It had been fairly easy to wine and dine her straight back to my hotel room.

We had a very enjoyable night there, and I learned just why the term Latin Lover applied as equally to women as it did to men. In the morning, I replaced her sunglasses with the pair I brought, complete with tracking and listening devices built in. Things had been going great, and I discovered that Senorita Sanchella herself, was the hired thief.

Then, last night, I had made the biggest mistake of my life. I went back to that damn bar.

Okay, it was my fault for having one drink too many, but when the local Don Juan had insulted the US, I lost my temper. What started out as a loud discussion, soon turned into a brawl, and when I left the bar at high speed, at least one or two of the locals lie dead. I knew that the Policia here were notorious for their torture methods, and in order to avoid them, I headed toward the Presidential compound, where I found Tereza getting into her car. She saw me and ushered me over.

She had seen my face on the TV, and because she had been seen with me, she was in fear for her own life. She had retrieved the stolen diamonds from their hiding place, and was hastily leaving town.

That was last night.

We drove to the ruins of Machu Picchu, the holiest of places in these parts, and I had called in an extraction. The problem was, when the extraction team arrived, they had opened fire on us.

With the deepest regret, I killed all four of them.

It seems I had been disavowed. The C.I.A. would already have destroyed all records of my mission, and were probably even now staging a tragic public death somewhere.

Ah well, it's only 350 km to the Port of Paracas, Tereza is very attractive, and it's amazing the kind of friends that 5 million dollars' worth of diamonds can buy.

I think I'm going to rather enjoy being a ghost.

Father Christmas

Lynn White

I was so excited.
It was nearly Christmas
and I was going to meet
Father Christmas himself.

I was so excited,
wearing my best coat and bonnet,
hopping from one foot to the other
in the long queue of children
waiting with their mums
to be allowed into Santa's Grotto.

I was so excited.
We were nearly there.
I could see the grotto
with it's tinsel and fairy lights
twinkling.
I was going to sit on his knee
and have my picture taken,
and that was in an age when
photographs were even rarer
than Christmases..

I was so excited.
There were the elves...
But wait..
they were cardboard.
Where were the real elves,
the magic ones,
why weren't they there?
"They're much too busy",
my mum said.
"But Father Christmas will be real".

We paid our money
and there he was.
He really was.
I couldn't wait to climb on his knee
and examine his beard.
I'd never seen a beard before.
But he was very tetchy when I pulled at it
and told me to stop.
Then it went lop sided
and I realised
it was a false beard

and I told him so, angrily.
He put it back.
"Stop thy wriggling", he said.
"You're not the real one,
I don't want to sit on your knee"

Flash went the camera.

And outside there was a queue of children
Waiting to be addressed.
Hands on hips.
"He's not the real one.
He's got a false beard.
He's not magic at all,
they're cheating you!"
It's a swiz!
Then the store manager came..

I was so excited.

First published by Silver Birch Press,

Me As A Child Series, May 2015

Keep On

Michelle Murray

Keep On
Keeping On
All it takes is one step
One day
One moment
Stay the course

Let the storm tossed waves
Shake, Splash, Roll
Let the wind howl
Blow
Stay the course

Let your ship
Guide you home
Let the wood moan
Break, Crack, Creak
Stand there defiant and brave
And stay the course.

Inertia

Ben Graham

Rest. The next ten minutes.

Sleep. The next eight hours.

Inertia. The next twenty years.

9:45 am

Waking slowly, you stretch out in the cool winter light. The bed's empty but for you. You can hear her downstairs, already getting started on the dinner. You lie there, chasing the lingering notes of a song you heard in a dream.

The house is warm. Too warm. It's stifling. The seasonal scents of the house mingle with the smell of cooking emanating from the kitchen. Cinnamon, chestnuts, pine needles and roasting meats. You can't escape it; a festive bouquet that reaches into every corner of the room to lap against the cold windows before rolling back on itself in a tidal rhythm.

On the landing, you wipe the condensation from the window and peer outside at the tiny backyard, a green carpet of grass glistening under crystalline frost. An iron blanket stretches over the sky. No snow today. It'll probably come in February when everyone is well and truly beyond the desire for snow. Peering at the frigid world beyond the window, you wonder when the garden became so overgrown.

You take a deep breath of warm air and descend the stairs.

Norah Jones on the kitchen speakers. The place is a hive, buzzing with the brouhaha of the annual dance. Pots simmer on the stove and jars of jams, jellies and chutneys sit open on the worktop. In the oven, a whole chicken roasts, stuffed with sage, breadcrumbs and walnuts. On the shelf below, cloves of garlic nestle between fluffed potatoes that sizzle in goose fat. She doesn't even look up from the cookbook when you walk in.

"Can I help?"

"You can glaze the carrots and parsnips"

You look around, irritated you even asked.

"Where are they?"

"Over by the oven. They just need honey but don't put them in yet." She still hasn't looked up.

She's in a mood. Probably because you came home so late last night. She knew you would do that. After this long together, she knows there's no such thing as '*one* at the pub'.

Still, you feel betrayed.

She said nothing when you left last night. Perhaps she knew it wouldn't make any difference. But, if she knows you well enough to understand that, surely she understands it's the one night you get to see your friends. You couldn't tell her the real reason you had to see them last night.

"Can I . . . ?" you trail off. You know better than to dismiss yourself.

"Sure," she says, her voice neutral. She still hasn't looked up.

12:30 pm

You sit with an unopened beer, the bottle perspiring in its transition from the cold fridge to the doughy warmth of the living room. You glance at the clock. 12:30. *Why not? It's OK today; anything goes for one day only.*

You call through to the kitchen: "I'm just gonna crack a beer. Why don't you come through and open your presents before your parents get here?"

Silence.

You can already imagine her face. She hates having conversations from different rooms. She calls through in a strained tone, "I've got a schedule to stick to if you want to eat before New Year."

You think of walking through, of taking her by the hand, of grabbing her waist, pulling her in close and kissing her soft, warm lips. You think of putting on *War Is Over* and dancing around the room as you both giggle, awkwardly watching your feet to avoid her toes, glancing up to find her looking into your eyes, a wry smile curving the tip of her mouth. You consider it, but the moment has gone and you know it. *She'll just assume you're trying to make up for something, She'll know something isn't right.* When did this all become so muted? When did interaction with this person become a chore?

You look up at the tree, as it stands blinking in the corner, festooned in a patchwork of purple and gold. The lights glimmer like cars on the horizon of some dark hill, rising and falling in bright rotations. The presents beneath are piled on a bright red rug, set down to catch the needles as they slowly break free. Your eye is drawn to the two stars, precariously perched atop.

A gift, from her, for your first Christmas together. Your mind circles back to that first flat, with its uneven walls, minuscule kitchen and mould in the bathroom. You recall the first time you sat down together to exchange gifts, the giddy expectation of the unknowable, with all the incredible possibilities it entailed.

Rest. The next ten minutes.

1:00 pm

You sit watching the TV. The same old crap as always, oddly comforting in its predictability. You wile away the time watching an old James Bond film. You chuckle at the terrible puns and wonder why you never found Honor Blackman attractive when you were younger. *They couldn't make a film like this today.* You feel ashamed for enjoying such archaic indulgence while she's sweating herself silly in the kitchen. Simultaneously, you can feel the heavy heat of the room pulling you down, deeper and deeper, into a world without foundations, without anchors, where routine and obligation take no precedent.

Sleep. The next hour.

You hear the ringtone of your phone. *Where is it?* You look around but you know it's not in the room with you.

"Your phone is ringing!" she calls through from the kitchen. You clamber from your seat and sprint through, then slow down so she doesn't see you running. You walk in casually, straining to contain the anxious frenzy in your voice.

You grab the phone and check the number. "It's work,"

you mutter with a shake of the head.

She sounds incredulous: "Today? They can't call you today."

You shrug in submission and scuttle through to the living room. The voice on the other end is a burst of ebullience.

"Merry Christmas, honey. You all ready for tonight?"

"I-I-I. Yes." You don't sound convinced, so you try to add something more reassuring. "I can't wait." You've spent the morning trying to push this from your mind. You know it's happening, but you're still not prepared to face it.

"Good. I can't wait! Boxing Day in the Bahamas. It's gonna be a dream come true." The enthusiasm in her voice makes you smile, even as it sets your heart racing.

"It will, but I have to go now. She's already suspicious."

"Oh," she sounds put out. *She was expecting more.*

"Look, I'll meet you tonight when she goes to bed." You can feel her waiting on the other end of the line. "I love you."

"I love you too."

You hang up, shame, glee and anticipation colliding in the pit of your stomach.

3:15 pm

You sit on the living room floor. She's perched on the faux fur rug in front of the fire. She sets out her presents with precision. She's already laid yours out before you.

George Michael sings about Last Christmas.

You both grin awkwardly.

She looks down and counts. "Well, you got me a few more this year, so I'll start."

She unravels the wrapping paper, taking care not to tear it. Another little quirk you used to think was cute.

She pulls out a book. The new Paula Hawkins.

She leans across and kisses you. "Thank you, I know I asked you to get it, but I'm glad you remembered this year."

You ignore the dig about last year and grab the present in front of you, shredding the paper with your fingernails. If she didn't want you to tear it, she would give you the good wrapping paper. *Aftershave.* The same one you get every year. You try to think of a joke you haven't used before, a witty rejoinder to this unspoken tradition, but your mind is a blank. You look up and grin, then crawl over to give her a kiss.

And so it goes, the slow, silent unwrapping. She repeats the process: unwrap, smile, "thank you", and kiss.

You reach your last present. So far, you've known about every gift months in advance. But this one is different. It's just smaller than a shoebox, wrapped in brown paper, tied with a string bow. You try not to look too perplexed. She smiles with what looks like nervous anticipation.

You take care unwrapping this one, pulling the knot gently undone. You unfold the paper from around the box and stare at the contents. *A camera.* You look up, confused.

"Well, you've been saying about how you want to get into photography for so long. I spent a long time talking to the man in the shop. I even looked at all the reviews online..."

She's babbling now. Nervous in the shadow of your

silence. A hot shame floods your body and burns your face. You try not to look at her. *Just keep staring at the box.* You can't even remember the last time you mentioned photography, but you know you've brought it up before.

You look up into her bright, animated eyes. You shake your head and smile, then shuffle toward her on your knees. She stops talking as you pull her in tight and rest your head on her shoulder.

"It's amazing, thank you so much," you whisper. It really is. You want to hug her forever, to reassure her, to let her know she deserves so much more than you. You clutch her tighter and try to push everything from your mind but her. You only let go when you hear the knock at the door.

Rest. The next three hours.

7:30 pm

You stand in the open front door, arm around her, waving her parents off as they reverse down the driveway. You can feel all the heat escaping from the house behind you. When they're gone, you both shuffle back into the warm belly of the house. She squeezes your hand and smiles.

"Thank you, you were really good this year."

You shrug with a smile. "I didn't even say anything when he started talking about Brexit."

"I know they're not the easiest to get along with, especially after *he's* had a drink."

Why is she being so nice today? Of course, if you're only going to be nice for one day of the year, it makes sense you would choose this day, but her affection is so sincere it's unnerving.

You follow her into the kitchen and begin filling the dishwasher.

"Don't forget my sister and Al will be here tomorrow, so please take the non-alcoholic beer out the fridge in the garage."

Of course, Al and Jean. The only two people who can suck the fun out of drinking. Then it hits you. *Tomorrow.* The creeping shame begins to churn in you again.

Now's the time to talk to her. But what can you say that you've never said before? What can you say that won't open a room in your relationship that you've worked so hard to keep locked? You look at her again and try to picture what it would be like to tell her. Today is the longest you've gone without arguing in months.

Is this cowardice, or just practical thinking? If you start down this route, you could be here for hours, just arguing. You can feel your lungs pulling in the air, your tongue forming the words, the peaceful calm climbing, higher, higher, ready to drop and shatter. You can sense the threads unravelling; the house, the car, the comfort, the security. It's the same reason you didn't tell work. You couldn't face the reality of it all. But now that you're aware of how open this all is, you can't get it out of your head. It's like an itch. *You need to tell her.*

You touch her arm. "Hey." She turns and smiles but her face drops when she sees your expression. *Don't say it.*

"What's up?" she asks. Her face is soft but you can hear the sharpness creeping into her tone.

Why ruin this moment? Why send this day into a nosedive when you're so close to landing? You could lay it all out now, tell her it's been great, but now it's time to move on.

You realise you've been quiet for too long.

"I love you," you stutter.

> *Inertia. The next twenty years.*

9:45 pm

How do you say goodbye to someone without telling them you're leaving?

The question circulates through your head like oxygen in the blood. You can't push it from your mind as you sit on the sofa, eyes fixed on the TV, your arm around her.

Before you realise you're speaking, you hear yourself say, "Do you remember when I first asked you out?" Afterwards, you sit there, dumbfounded at your audacity. All of this will seem like a cruel joke tomorrow.

She will recall it through tears to her sister, cursing herself for not reading deeper into your unprovoked nostalgia.

"Erm," she looks puzzled, "yeah. It was the freshers' party and you were there with your friend, what's his name—"

"Paul."

"Yeah, you were downing all those free ciders, and you offered me one . . ." She trails off, embarrassed despite the fact that you're her only audience.

"And I asked what you were studying and pretended I was on the same course," you laugh.

"And you kept it up all night."

"Well, until you started asking me about Milan Canada."

"*Kundera.*"

You blush and try not to let her correction throw you off, but it's gone. In the silence that sets in, you hear Fairytale of New York playing quietly over the TV.

"Right, Kundera. They're all the same, those French philosophers."

"Czech," she says with a grin. "And he wasn't . . ." she trails off. She knows you get the point.

"Whatever happened to us?" You don't even realise you've said it until you see the look on her face.

"Erm," she stutters. "Well, we grew up. I don't know, we just . . ." She feels around for the words. "We just didn't stay the same. You realise that life isn't going to give you everything you dreamed of, and you begin to appreciate just having the little things; a roof over your head, a paycheck at the end of the month, someone to be there when you need them. That's how it is, I guess."

You both sit in silence for a while. Her blunt assessment of your shared evolution has pulled you back into reality with such force you're startled to find yourself sitting there, with Shane MacGowan and the ghost of Kirsty MacColl still singing away.

"Do you remember our first Christmas?"

"Of course," you laugh, grateful she's willing to resuscitate the conversation. "In that tiny flat on Lincoln Road."

"You bought that huge tree and had to cut it in half just to make it fit."

"That's right, and we bought two trees worth of decorations." Your eyes flit to the two stars sat atop the tree.

"I like our little traditions. I hope we're still doing them when we're eighty."

You proffer a convincing smile but the reference to the future sticks like a thistle in your throat.

"Anyway," she says, standing. "I'm going to bed, I'm absolutely exhausted." She kisses you on the head. "Don't be too late to bed."

"I won't."

She stops at the door and smiles. "Merry Christmas, baby. I had a really nice day."

The words stir a clenching shame in your stomach. One more lie, just one more. "Me too darling. I'll be up soon."

She leaves you sitting in silence. Your stare at the tree again, unsure of what to do next.

The boys from the NYPD Choir are still singing Galway Bay.

Rest. The next hour.

12:00 am

The doubts come creeping in like water over the side of a capsizing boat. The steadfast resolution of this morning has been eroded by beer, food, and the idiotic illusion that today represents some kind of new start, a new normal.

But then maybe it could be. After all, if you believe what the world tells you, this should be enough. *Why isn't this enough?* You think about the dreams she sacrificed to be here too. She was going to be an interior designer.

But then life happens and ambitions take a backseat to reality; the annual holidays, the monthly bills, the daily grind.

22 years. The slow choke. Like a band around the finger, cutting off the circulation. Every day, you feel the cyclic routine grip tighter - the blood slowly draining, the cells, deprived of oxygen, withering and dying.

Never had kids. She told you she wasn't interested in them. You knew she always harbored a warm, abstract kind of yearning for a life beyond her own. You knew she stopped the pill. Still, despite your casual attitude to protection, she never conceived. Maybe it was you. Maybe all those years of drinking and smoking decimated your *little troops*. Would you want to stay if the house was filled with the laughter of children? Perhaps that would have bonded you two better, united under the shared drudgery of parental responsibility.

None of that matters. It doesn't matter what kind of day you had. It doesn't matter that this will break her. It doesn't matter that it would be easier to sit right here, then crawl into bed, and forget any of this ever happened. For once in your life, you need to make a decision that's right for *you* and stick to it.

You realise you haven't written the letter yet. *The fucking letter.* The letter to explain all of this. A few sheets of paper to put an end to everything you've built, everything you've allowed to fester in you without realizing.

You sit down with the paper. You can't remember the last time you wrote a letter. What can you say? Why are you only thinking of this now? It's not like you to leave this until the last moment. Then again, none of this is like you. It's not like you to make a life-changing decision and stick to it. And look where that's landed you. The same street, the same house, the same person.

Rest. The next ten minutes.

1:30 am

The house is quiet. You can feel the foundations groaning as if they know a seismic shift is about to take place. The walls creak, taut with expectation, willing you to rise from the armchair and begin the final phase.

Some things you left where they were. The charger by the bed, the book you were only half-finished. The clothes you packed aren't your favourite, but that's a necessity. You check the bag. Clothes, passport, laptop. It's surprising how much of the last ten years can be contained in a small backpack. You check your pockets. Phone, wallet, a pack of cigarettes. You don't smoke anymore, but you'll need one. Your fingers alight on your keys. You want to leave them but worry the metallic clink will create too much noise. She won't need them anyway.

You leave the camera, as much as it pains you. Part of you hopes she will use it, grow to love it, make a career out of it, host her own exhibitions, so that in a way this was the right decision for both of you. *She'll probably return it.*

You creep through the house on tiptoes, taking your coat and shoes from the cupboard beneath the stairs. In the living room, you decide to leave the lights on when you leave. As you walk out, you look up at the two stars and see them glimmer.

Standing in the hallway, your fingers grip the door handle. *You can't back out now.* You open the door gently, taking care to steady your breathing.

You hoist the bag onto your back and step out into the freezing cold.

The streets are empty. Of course, who would be out tonight?

The pavements glint with millions of frost particles and the air is sharp as if charged with a current that pinches at your face. You look up at the cloudless night sky but only a few stars are visible under the luminous blanket of orange streetlights. You realise that you'll never experience this again, the sensation of being utterly alone, leaving behind an empire of comforts, memories and habituated living. The world is callously unpredictable, but you've carved out a comfortable nest in which to shelter from the chaos. In leaving your nest — in fact, abandoning it altogether — you open yourself up to the mercies of a world you can never fully understand.

You reach the street corner where she said she'd meet you. No car yet. You sit on a low garden wall and check the time. *1:35.* You rub your hands together to fight the cold creeping into your fingertips and realise you're still wearing your ring. You take it off and pocket it. It's too much to just throw it. Minutes pass. You check your phone, then check it again when you realise you weren't even looking the first time.

3:30 am

You jump on the spot, willing the warmth into your body. *Where is she?* You've called her phone six times, sent her four messages. You've missed the flight anyway. You know she isn't coming but you can't bring yourself to accept it.

After all, you made the leap, you walked out of that house and didn't look back. She didn't even have anything to leave behind, at least not as much as you.

A thought hits you. You pull your phone and check the news; nothing. You check the traffic updates. There's been an accident on the M40. Expect delays. That's all it says.

You know you're just being foolish. She's probably at home, asleep, wondering what on earth she was thinking, running off with a married man. Hot shame floods your face again. *How could you be so stupid?* You stand, but you can't take your eyes from the silver light of the phone screen. You search Twitter, the local news sites.

And there it is. The car. *Her car.* A crumpled mass of metal and plastic, metallic Carolina blue.

The headline reads: '*Multiple fatalities in M40 crash*'.

You realise with disgust that the first feeling is relief — she was coming. You knew she wouldn't leave you. But now the reality begins to set in. Your face is cold. You shake your head, slowly at first, then with all the violence and anger you can summon. *No.* This isn't real. None of this is real. You look up at the sky, still black and empty. You can hear a sound, like a high-pitched tremor. You look up and down the empty street but there's no-one, and that's when you realise the sound is coming from you.

You walk back up the street, shivering, inwardly cursing, furious that you ever believed this existence you've painted yourself into could ever change. Your head spins and you have to stop to lean against a wall. Before you can react, your stomach heaves up hot, bitter bile. You fall to your knees, still clutching the wall, crying, screaming, trying to spit the fury from your body but it won't leave; your body just keeps producing it until you feel like there's nothing left in you but desperate useless anger. The sweat on your forehead from the violent spasms begins to cool and clasps your brain in a freezing grip.

Finally, you stand up, suck the cold air deep into your lungs and try to deny your body the luxury of shivering. You retrace your steps back to the house. A thousand thoughts flit through your numb mind. You'll tear up the letter. Burn it. You'll stash your clothes too. *Then what?* How are you going to face Al and Jean tomorrow? You can't even tell anyone. That's the thing with keeping something like this to yourself — there's no one to tell when it all falls apart. And it always does. The adventure was doomed before you even started. And now *she's* gone, your only hope for a reprieve — the vague light in grey darkness, extinguished.

You look up and realise you're standing at the bottom of the driveway. You inhale and taste vomit on your tongue. Through the window you see the two stars glistening atop the tree, signaling your way home.

You feel the alcohol and the warmth and the familiarity of the day, of the whole place, grip your body. It feels like a lifetime ago that you stepped outside this bubble.

You lay down on the doorstep, exasperated, grief-stricken, exhausted.

Rest. The next ten minutes.

Sleep. The next eight hours.

Inertia. The next 20 years.

Window and Glass

Ron Wilson

Mandy and I were friends.

Fridays at 4:40 became the highlight of my week, as we caught up on each other's lives. Her, behind the glass talking into a thin microphone; me sitting in my car, breathing the faint smell of exhaust and heat-soaked concrete.

It was weird, our friendship.

We didn't ever go clubbing together, or out to eat. Never hugged or even shook hands. We weren't even friends on Facebook. I only ever saw her through the bank's drive up window. But . . .

Damn this is hard.

I mean we shared things with each other that nobody else ever knew about. Ours was a relationship that actually *flourished* on three minutes a week. I can honestly say she is—*was*—my best friend. I'll never have another like her.

The day we met she smiled at me through the glass. It was festooned with big fuzzy spiders and fake webs. A little witch on a broomstick hovered from one corner.

She looked at the deposit slip and asked me if I worked for Palmer Construction.

"Yes, I'm their new bookkeeper."

"Well, congratulations!" She said. "They're a sweet bunch." She leaned into the glass a little and lowered her voice. "Must be nice hanging around all those hot construction guys."

I assured her I had no idea what she was talking about and we laughed together.

But honestly, I could never figure out where Mandy got the idea that I worked with a bunch of *sweet guys*. Or attractive ones for that matter. Unless a trophy gut, body odor and breath redolent of stale beer and fast food was her idea of a good time.

Roger Palmer was the exception. A Daniel Craig look-alike, he was single *and* he drove a Mercedes convertible.

"What's it like to work for Mr. Palmer?" Mandy asked.

I furrowed my brow and tried to look severe. Then I spoke as deeply as I could manage, trying to imitate him.

"Julie, I want you to take this to First National Bank after work. Leave here at 4:30. Take South Street to Gordon, that way you won't get hung up by a train. And watch out for the

school zone. And remember to breathe in, and then breathe out, and if your butt itches, don't scratch it until you're sure no one is looking."

Mandy was giggling.

"A bit of a micro-manager," I said. "But he seems nice enough, so far."

"Yeah, he has a reputation for being quite the *type-A* personality," Mandy said.

"No kidding, but it's his *body* type that caught my attention."

"Looks like that guy that plays James Bond, right?"

I rolled my eyes and smiled. She smiled back. And just like that . . . we were friends.

It was the same every Friday. Roger tossed a blue zippered pouch on my desk, and I went to visit Mandy.

~

"Oh my God Julie! It's *beautiful*," Mandy said, gazing at my tennis bracelet through the glass. The spider and webs had been replaced by a piñata and a small Mexican flag. A green, white and red banner declared Happy Cinco de Mayo.

"Thanks," I said.

"You say *Roger* bought it for you?"

"He gave it to me for my six-month anniversary with the company."

"Mm-hmm," Mandy said with a tone that implied she knew there was more to the story than I was letting on. She leaned in close to the window and whispered; I always found it cute the way she did that, like her voice wasn't coming through the little speaker, but through the glass.

"Be careful Julie. There's something . . . menacing about him sometimes."

"You're just jealous Mandy," I said, smiling. But I didn't feel like smiling, because I knew she was right. There *was* something menacing about him. It was a feeling I had been repressing for weeks. A feeling that would pop up every now and then, threatening to ruin an evening.

I got good at using a mental club to beat those feelings into submission. Smack 'em back down where they belonged. Down somewhere deep, where I couldn't see or hear their stupid accusations.

Like psychological whack-a-mole.

Whack. Whack. Whack.

The thing is, he was never *not* a perfect gentleman. He never forced me to do anything I didn't want to. Never threatened me. Never raised his voice to me. Yes, he was very demanding when it came to work; he is a meticulous man.

So those feelings I would get—the *menacing* feelings— had no right to be there. No reason to exist.

They came more frequently, the longer we dated. It would be a look, or a quick clenching of his jaw, or closing of his fist. Sometimes it was just a sharp edge to his voice, so quick and indistinct that I could never decide if it were him, or my imagination.

Whack. Whack. Whack.

~

A week after Roger gave me the tennis bracelet, he called me into his office. I told Mandy the whole story. In less than three minutes of course.

I told her that Palmer Construction had serious tax problems. I told her how Roger confided in me. How he had named off the individual children of his employees, and their medical issues, and their financial needs.

"He really cares about his people," I said.

It was all true. Zoe Miller needed physical therapy, and little Jimmy Parke had leukemia. Stan Wannamaker and his wife were in the process of adopting a little girl from Romania.

"If he goes out of business, the guys would lose their jobs, *and* their health plans," I said. "Just think about all those families."

"He could always sell his Mercedes," she said, her voice flat. "Or maybe his Porsche." Then she sighed. "I'm sorry; that was mean. So, what're you going to do?"

I told her I was . . . *helping* him.

She leaned into the window. "You're what? How? . . ." Her eyes widened as she whispered, "*Cooking the books?*"

"I have to do something. The kids, remember?"

"You're not really going to *fall* for that are you?"

She was right of course. If the sob story about the kids had come from anyone but my Roger, I wouldn't have believed it.

I know it was crazy to confide criminal activity to a teller at my company's bank, but the window was our confessional. Sometimes I was the priest. Other times it was Mandy. We were friends, confidantes sworn to secrecy. Besides, Mandy's boss, Frank, already knew; not about how I was *helping,* but about the company's financial issues. He was Roger's banker, after all. Heck, he probably knew more than I did. More than Roger even.

Probably not more than the IRS though.

~

Roger kept up his opulent lifestyle. He used money borrowed from the bank, he used money that he owed to the government. I did some creative bookkeeping. We were a team, and it worked. Zoe got her physical therapy. Jimmy got his chemo. And the Wannamaker's little girl was adorable—hard to understand, but cute anyway.

A week later Frank, Mandy's boss, called in the Palmer Construction loan. That was the first day Roger scared me. While talking to Frank on his cell phone, he threw it into the computer monitor and started a small fire.

He screamed curses.

He punched a wall.

He said he would kill Frank.

Whack.

~

Red white and blue stars decorated the window.

"For the record Julie, I think you and Roger make a cute couple. A real-life *Ken and Barbie.* But . . ." Her face grew serious.

"But what?"

"Just watch yourself, Julie. He has a temper. You know Frank? The manager here?" She leaned towards the glass and whispered, *"I think he's afraid of Roger."*

"Roger's a sweetheart," I said.

Whack.

I drove away.

~

Roger didn't lose his cool for the next couple months. Mandy even commented on his change of personality. She told me he had dropped off gifts a couple times for Frank and his staff.

"Sherrie's Cherries, Julie. Can you believe it?"

I told her I could.

She leaned into the window. "Frank thinks he's desperate for a new loan. It'll never happen, but don't tell Roger. I *love* those things."

The sensible thing to do was quit both my job, and Roger. But by then I loved him. I loved his lifestyle. I had grown accustomed to luxury. If I knew what he was planning, I would have quit. Hell, I would have called the police.

Whack. Whack.

~

"You're kidding. Fiji? Really?" Mandy said. Fuzzy spiders and the miniature witch were back in their places. Mandy was dressed in a tight brown leather jacket with a longbow strung over her back.

"I think he might pop the question."

"That is so amazing Julie, but . . ." Mandy paused and looked around her space to see if she was alone. Frank was in the habit of coming out to say hi to me lately, interrupting our little three minute visits.

I cut her off. "Look, Mandy, I really love that we can talk. I love that I can tell you *anything*, but you don't know the whole story."

"Honey . . ." Here she leaned in close to the window and whispered. "What you're doing for him is, *really* dangerous."

She was right. That's why I was angry; I could end up in jail. *But I was doing it for the kids*. We lie best, to ourselves.

"Katniss Everdeen?" I said, changing the subject.

Her face lit up. "You're the first one to get it right. One guy thought I was going for Indiana Jones."

"You're not even wearing a fedora!"

"So, tell me more about your trip," Mandy said.

"Ten days of sun," I forced myself to sound cheery.

"When do you two leave?"

"Well, Roger has some meetings, so we're taking different flights. He goes Thursday, and I'll be leaving Saturday morning."

"So we won't have to miss our Friday chat," Mandy said, beaming with delight.

~

Before he left for Fiji, Roger left the familiar blue zippered pouch on my desk as usual. It sat next to a box of Sherrie's Cherries. There was a sticky note on the box.

Julie, the box of cherries is for Frank and his staff. Send it through with the deposit. See you Saturday.

(and don't forget to pack your bikini.)

The box might have seemed a little bigger—a little heavier—than usual; but I thought nothing of it.

Whack. Whack. Whack.

Mandy's eyes grew wide with excitement when I waved the box of Sherrie's Cherries in front of the window. I mimicked opening it but didn't. Mandy waggled a reproving finger at me. "Don't you *dare*. I get first pick," she said. We laughed and she called for Frank.

I placed the box and the bag in the drawer. The box barely fit.

"Frank, Julie brought a surprise," Mandy said.

I watched as Frank came to the window. He waved at me and asked how I had been as the drawer closed.

Mandy reached for the box. Frank grabbed it playfully before she could. I smiled at them as Frank started to open the seal with a letter opener.

"Julie, wait . . . don't leave without a cherry," Mandy said.

She leaned into the window like so many times before, like she wanted to tell me something secret while Frank was preoccupied.

Frank opened the box. A terrible flash of white light blinded me for a moment. The fake spider webs were instantly replaced by a million cracks that resembled them.

As it turns out, the window was bomb-proof safety glass. But it didn't help Mandy at all. Or Frank. Or any of the other five employees and seven customers.

Mandy's face . . . *pushed into* the glass.

When I could see again, Mandy was closer to me than ever before. Her brown eyes bulged and flattened against the glass. Her teeth, broken and jagged, pushed through her lips and made a contrast of red and white candy-cane colors. Her ears . . . I could see into them. They were both flat against the glass as well. Her face was . . . spread out. That's all I can say.

It was *spread out*.

Her hair burned. Flames shot all around, and I had the thought—the terrible thought—that if her limp body had still been attached to her head, it would surely have pulled her away from the glass.

Her face remained, though, and her hair burned.

And I drove away, screaming.

~

My feelings no longer warn me. Now they only mock me. I have long since dropped the mental club. I leave them be. I let them run their course as they jeer, tease, and abuse.

I speak to people through a different window now.

The thin microphone has been replaced with a grimy teller phone.

Sorry. Telephone.

The person on the other side is not Mandy. Not even a friend, but appointed to be there.

No decorations are allowed to adorn the glass, regardless of the season . . . and maybe that's a good thing.

Contributors

Authors, Artists and Poets Askew

Ed Ahern resumed writing after forty odd years in foreign intelligence and international sales. He's had over two hundred fifty stories and poems published so far, and five books. Ed works the other side of writing at Bewildering Stories, where he sits on the review board and manages a posse of six review editors.

https://twitter.com/bottomstripper
https://www.facebook.com/EdAhern73
https://www.instagram.com/edwardahern1860

Faith Maria Brody is a writer and producer of independent films. Her award winning film, *Miss December* was distributed through SModcast Productions. Her screenplay, *Scarlett Sunshine* is also an award winner, and was last featured in the 'DC Spotlight on Screenwriters' festival, which showcases women writers.

Kimberly Garrett Brown is the founder and executive editor of *Minerva Rising Press*. Her novel, *Cora's Kitchen* was a finalist in the *2018 William Faulkner – William Wisdom Creative Writing Competition* and the *2016 Louise Meriwether First Book Prize*. Her work has appeared in *Black Lives Have Always Mattered: A collection of essays, poems and personal narratives, The Feminine Collective, Compass Literary Magazine, Today's Chicago Woman, Chicago Tribune* and elsewhere. She has a MFA in Creative Writing from Goddard College.

www.minervarising.com
kimberlygarrettbrown.com

Steve Carr, who lives in Richmond, Virginia, has had over 350 short stories published internationally in print and online magazines, literary journals and anthologies since June, 2016. Five collections of his short stories, *Sand, Rain, Heat, The Tales of Talker Knock* and *50 Short Stories: The Very Best of Steve Carr,* have been published. His paranormal/horror novel *Redbird* is due out in late November, 2019. His plays have been produced in several states in the U.S. He has been nominated for a Pushcart Prize twice.

twitter.com/carrsteven960 (@carrsteven960)
www.stevecarr960.com
www.facebook.com/steven.carr.35977

Melodie Corrigall is an eclectic Canadian writer whose work has appeared in *Litro UK, Foliate Oak, Toasted Cheese, Emerald Bolts, Earthen Lamp Journal, Halfway Down the Stairs, Bethlehem Writers Roundtable, Corner Bar Magazine, Persimmon Tree, Literally Stories,* and *The Write Place at the Write Time.*

www.melodiecorrigall.com

Phil Gladden writes a weekly newspaper column published by *The Bourbon County Citizen,* in Paris Kentucky and he has a collection of those articles coming out soon. He has won first place in the *Harriet Rose Legacy* literary contest and was recognized in the *Green River Writers* contest. His essays have been published four times in *Good Ole Days Magazine,* as well as winning the *Penned* fiction contest in the *Kentucky Monthly.*

Ben Graham was born in the barren heartlands of Durham, England. His love of literature grew from reading the works of Joyce, Hemingway, Ginsberg and several other writers a teenage boy should really have no interest in reading. Following several years struggling to pay rent as a freelance journalist, Ben became a copywriter and editor for an architecture firm in Edinburgh. Ben now divides his time between writing, reading, and frequenting the drinking establishments of renowned Edinburgh authors in the hope of finding some clue to their genius or, failing that, a good dram of whisky.

Dusty Grein is the Managing Editor for Production and Design at Rhetoric Askew, an author, a poet and a graphics designer. His critically acclaimed novel, *The Sleeping Giant*, is available in print and as a Kindle Select title. His shorter works and poetry have been published in several collections. An award winning and A.C.P. accredited poet, he is a contributing member of *The Society of Classical Poets*, and a part of their Advisory Board. His how-to essays on creating classical-form poetry have appeared both online and in two of their annual collections. His blog, *From Grandpa's Heart...* is followed by fans around the world.

rhetaskewpublishing.com
dustygrein.wixsite.com/author
grandpasheart.blogspot.com

John Grey is an Australian poet, US resident. Recently published in *Front Range Review, Studio One* and *Columbia Review* with work upcoming in *Louisiana Review, Poem and Midwest Quarterly*.

Sarah Henry is a former student of two U.S, poet laureates at the University of Virginia. Today she lives near Pittsburgh, where her poems have appeared in the *Pittsburgh Post-Gazette*, the *Pittsburgh Poetry Review* and *The Loyalhanna Review*. Sarah's other publications include two *Anthologies Askew*, *Soundings East*, *The Hollins Critic* and three humor magazines, among many journals. She is retired from a newspaper.

Sandi Hoover is a geologist by training and naturalist by interest. She frequently writes about nature in the southwest, sharing observations and insights. Human emotions and their expression also intrigue her and stimulate stories. She is a member of the award winning *Corrales Writing Group*, and an award winning author in her own right. The wildlife outside their office windows entertain Sandi, her husband Richard, and Sophie, their indoor cat.

www.facebook.com/WritersInCorrales

Adam Johnson is a father, a nerd culture enthusiast, a student of personal development and a lifelong lover of story. Fantasy and science fiction are his chosen genres, but he likes to take any chance to blend genres and write outside of his comfort zone. Adam currently lives, works and writes in lower Michigan, but his favorite love story has drawn him to the South where he will soon call home.

Nerisha Kemraj is a short-fiction author and Poet, who resides in South Africa with her husband and two daughters. She has work published/accepted in 39 publications, both print and online. She holds a Bachelor's degree in Communication Science.

www.facebook.com/pg/Nerishakemrajwriter/
www.instagram.com/nerishakemraj (@nerishakemraj)

Laurie Kolp's poems have appeared in the *Southern Poetry Anthology VIII*: Texas, Moria, Stirring, Whale Road Review, Rust + Moth, and more. Her poetry books include the full-length Upon the Blue Couch and chapbook Hello, It's Your Mother. An avid runner and lover of nature, Laurie lives in Southeast Texas with her husband, three children, and two beautiful dogs.

Mandy Melanson is a stay-at-home mother of 3 home-schooled children who are the loves of her life. Mandy's passion for the written word began with the bedtime stories her mother would read to her. Her love for fictional worlds has traveled with her throughout her life. Mandy is the founder of *Rhetoric Askew* and *RhetAskew Publishing*. Her first chapbook, *The Mind of the Muse*, is available on Amazon. Her work can also be found in the *Our Write Side Anthology*.

www.facebook.com/groups/551246565025153

Michelle Murray is a working mother of two young adult children. She has been writing since high school. A number of her poems and short stories have been published in anthologies. She was also featured in *Who's Who Among American Poets*. She currently has a fantasy series published called *The Dream Walker, Land of Mystica* series. When not writing, she enjoys time with her family, the outdoors, and going for walks. You will usually find her with a notebook and pen sitting outside on a sunny day.

P.A. O'Neil's stories have been featured in multiple anthologies (many of them international best-sellers), on-line journals, and magazines. She resides in Olympia, Washington. For links to books which feature her stories, look under the Photo sections of her Facebook author page.

www.facebook.com/p.a.oneil.storyteller

Nikki Rohira was born and raised in Dhule, India, where she lives and works. She is described as a vibrant person with lots of questions, lots of inspiration, lots of smile and lots of love. She is a technical and web content writer at IntelliSoftware. Her love for reading and inspiring people makes her write, and besides writing SEO content for business, she creates literary, fiction and inspirational work, which you can find on her Instagram and Facebook accounts.

www.instagram.com/ink.pen.heart (@ink.pen.heart)
www.facebook.com/nikita.rohira
nikchik.blogspot.com

Kent Swarts is a retired aerospace engineer and amateur astronomer. He has edited the clubs news letter for 13 years, and has stories published in three anthologies, as well as online. He lives in Waco, TX.

Jim Tritten is a retired Navy pilot living in a semi-rural village in New Mexico with his Danish artist/author wife, and their four cats. He has won numerous awards for his writing.

www.amazon.com/author/jimtritten
www.facebook.com/jimtrittenauthor
www.goodreads.com/author/show/2487183.James_John_ Tritten

Wim Verveen started his career in biology before he pursued a career in IT. He has written many articles for magazines IT related subjects. He likes to write stories with a mix of technology, fantasy and a touch of horror with a surprising twist. Wim lives in the Netherlands.

Patricia Walkow is an award-winning author. Her work was honored in the *2016 William Faulkner Literary Competition*. A full-length biography, *The War Within, the Story of Josef*, won first place awards in national and international competitions. She writes short stories and essays and has contributed to both online and in-print anthologies, newspapers, and magazines. The most recently anthology she contributed to and edited, *Love, Sweet to Spicy*, won a 2019 1st place award from *New Mexico Press Women* and 2nd place from *National Federation of Press Women*. Ms. Walkow was a former systems manager in a Fortune 200 company, edited *Corrales MainStreet News* for three years, and is a member of the *Corrales Writing Group*. She lives in Corrales, New Mexico with her husband, cats, and one very spoiled dog.

walkowconsulting.com

Lynn White lives in north Wales. Her work is influenced by issues of social justice and events, places and people she has known or imagined. She is especially interested in exploring the boundaries of dream, fantasy and reality. Her poem 'A Rose For Gaza' was shortlisted for the *Theatre Cloud 'War Poetry for Today'* competition 2014. She has been nominated for a Pushcart and her poems have appeared in many publications including: *Apogee, Firewords, Indie Soleil, Light Journal, Snapdragon* and *So It Goes Journal*.

lynnwhitepoetry.blogspot.com
www.facebook.com/Lynn-White-Poetry-1603675983213077

Ron Wilson's former life has prepared him for his current writing career. Having lived out hundreds of real-life adventures in places that range from the Rocky Mountains, to the Arizona Desert, to the Gulf Coast of Texas, he has a deep well of experience that comes alive in his works of fiction. Having an insatiable curiosity and a flair for seeing just how wrong things can go are two of the three reasons his writing is fun. Being able to make the reader see it is the third.

Maxwell Zwain writes flash fiction, short stories, novellas and movie reviews for his blog. He loves superhero stories and trading card games.

zwainmoviereviews.wordpress.com